Praise for Rachel Dove

"Frothy, funny and entertaining throughout, Nice Guys Finish Lonely offers a satisfying hug in a novel about our most important relationships. The characters and plot are engaging, and it'll make you look at nice guys differently by the end. Definitely a book that deserves to be read in one sitting from an author whose voice is welcomed in fiction." -*Áine Toner, author of Lets Talk About Six*

"Rachel Dove knows how to capture the reader's attention and it's easy to become lost in her writing. This story brought tears to my eyes and also made me laugh out loud, and it has some of the best one-liners I've ever come across!' – *Darcie Boleyn, author of Summer at Conwenna Cove*

"Frequently charming, occasionally heart-breaking, endlessly witty… my favourite read this year." - *Peter Jones*, author of *My Girlfriend's Perfect Ex-Boyfriend*

Manatee Books

First published in 2018.

This book is primarily a work of fiction. Other names, characters, businesses, organisations, places and events are the product of the authors imagination or are used fictitiously. Any resemblance to actual persons, living or dead, events or locales is entirely coincidental.

Published by Manatee Books

Paperback ISBN: 978-1-912347-10-0
Kindle ISBN: 978-1-912347-11-7

Cover design by Aimee Coveney of Bookollective
Images used under licence from Shutterstock.com

Nice Guys Finish Lonely

This Book
Belongs
To
Katie

Rachel Dove

To
Katie

Happy reading!

R Dove

RACHEL DOVE
x

ManateeBooks

This book is dedicated to all the Rory's out there – being overlooked by the right and wrong women, in favour of the bad boys. Guys, keep being you. If she's worth it, she will wake up one day. As they say, ruin a woman's lipstick, never her mascara.

To my boys, J & N
Never be a Greg, always be a Rory. There are plenty of Gregs out there, but the Rory type is the one to be, the one for a girl to long for. Cardigans and all. Always be yourself, never change for anyone. I found my Rory. I think you know him. You call him Daddy. Our very own spectacled superhero.

Love you

Mum

Xxxx

CHAPTER ONE

30 years ago

The room Rory's mother sleeps in has a funny smell. It does smell like her, but there's something else here too. Something he can't name in his head. It makes him wrinkle his nose when he comes in. His dad pushes the little boy forward with a gentle shove, and he slowly pads across the thick cream carpet to her bed. One sock flaps off his right foot, hanging there haphazardly. It says Tuesday on it. He knows it's Saturday, because Dad's home. His mum always looked after his socks before, and they always matched the day. Rory looks back to the doorway, but his dad has gone, closing the door. Trapping the aroma in with them both. The smell cloys around the boy's nostrils, making his nose twitch. He looks back at his mother, and she is looking straight at him. Her long blonde hair has been brushed by the nurse and is fanned out on the white pillows she is laid on. She looks like the angel they put on the top of their Christmas tree. Her head and arms are above the thick flowered quilt, and the rest of her tiny body is wrapped up underneath. She lifts up her arms, and Rory flinches at the wires coming from her. She says it's to put medicine into her body to kill the bugs, but he doesn't think it's working very well. She has been in bed for a long time. She lifts them a little higher and wiggles her fingers at her son. Rory remembers when she used to do that at the school gates, squatting down and hugging her knees to her chest. Throwing her arms out wide for him to run into with a squeal. He does it now but remembers what the nurse says. Gentle, gentle. He hops up onto the bed and slots himself into her arms.

'Hi Bear,' she croaks at him. 'Oh, you feel so big.' She rubs her hand round in circles on his back, like she always does. It feels different today though. She doesn't do it as hard anymore.

'I still fit though!' Rory protests, as she tucks him into her body. 'We fit together, like puzzle pieces. See. Click!'

His mother laughs feebly. 'That's right my little Rory Bear, we still fit together. Click click!' She taps his nose with a shaky finger and he giggles. She smiles at him, pulling him close to her and dropping kisses all over his face. Rory squirms a little, but really, he loves it.

'Are you going to get up soon?' He asks, picking up the locket that hangs from her chest. He likes to look at the pictures inside. She takes it from her neck and looks at it in her palm.

'Rory, I need to speak to you, and I want you to listen, okay?' Her face has changed now, from happy to sad, and Rory feels an odd sensation in the pit of his stomach. He nods at his mum, his big brown eyes focusing on her own watery ones. She hugs him tight and takes a deep shaky breath. 'You know Mummy has been sick, and in bed?'

Rory nods sadly, and his mother pushes away a tear that spills over onto her pale cheek.

'Well, the doctors say that the medicine isn't working, so I'll have to leave soon, to live in heaven, with your grandad.'

Rory looks to the window, where he can see the clouds slowly moving across the bright blue sky outside. 'Up there?' He asks, pointing. His mum nods.

'Yes, up there to sit on the clouds. I will be with my Dad and watch you live here with your daddy.'

Rory starts to cry, little sobs at first, then bigger as the pain in his chest gets worse. 'I don't want you to go Mummy, stay!' His mum pulls him to her, squeezing him as tight as she is able.

'I have to go, Rory Bear, but listen, I want you to do something for me. I want you to be a good boy, and when you grow up, I want you to be a good man, too. Mummy is so proud of you, and so is Daddy.'

Rory buries his face into his mum's neck. The smell is stronger here, it makes his mum's perfume smell funny. She pulls away, opening the locket and showing it to him. Inside are two photographs, one of him and one of her.

'This is yours now, and when you meet the woman you love more than any other, give it to her, from me and from you. Remember, Rory, treat women better than your father does. You have to be a good man, a man a woman can trust and depend on. A man who will look after her and love her no matter what. Do you understand, Rory Bear?'

Rory looks at the two photos in the locket, the pair of faces in there together forever. He wipes his tears and takes a big shuddery sigh. 'I will be a good man, I promise, Mummy.'

His mum smiles then, a big open smile, and then she lays back against the pillows. She looks tired, so Rory pulls the quilt up around her. She reaches for him, but her arms slip back limply by her sides. He puts the locket around his neck, looking at the pictures in their silver case as he snuggles into her side. He settles into the crook of her arm, feeling his warmth mingle with hers. He wishes he could keep her. He knows Grandad will look after her, but Rory needs her too. He thinks about what she said, about Daddy. He made Mummy sad sometimes, before she got sick. Now, he just cried a lot, spent a lot of time at work, or on the phone at home. His mother is asleep now, he can feel her breathing next to him. He looks out the window at the clouds. He thinks of his mum sitting on one watching him, checking he is a good man. He kisses his mum on the cheek, before falling asleep laid in her embrace.

CHAPTER TWO

Present Day

Friday

It is a truth universally acknowledged that a man watching a girl in a nightclub is either a jealous ex, a creepy stalker, or a man in love. Rory Gallant was the latter, and he had been for as long as he could remember. The object of his affection? Jessica Rabbit. Well, not actually Jessica Rabbit, but the human non-cartoon version of her. Sasha Birkenstock, the girl who looked like the dresses were assembled around her shapely body, rather than her being poured into them. Her red hair flamed atop her perfectly made up face, and when she walked through Miranda's nightclub, the sea of revellers parted for her. The occasional drunk even lay at her high heeled feet, like a fallen tribute. Sasha would just sashay past them, bestowing the odd friendly smile here and there, blowing air kisses like magic dust around the club. Rory nursed his bottle of water to his chest, following her progress across the floor intently. He felt a tap on his shoulder and stood away from his position leaning against the bar to look behind him. Sarah was sticking bottles into the bottle opener in quick succession, passing them over the busy bar and taking crisp notes from the punters. She was also shaking her head and rolling her eyes at him.

'What?' he said, over the early evening music. Later, the decibels would rise, and the beats would come thicker and faster, as the clientele turned into the heavier drinking dance crowd. She kept serving people, smiling and taking orders. Sarah never missed a beat. Some bar staff came here thinking it would be fun, and crumpled under the social pressure, the noise and the sheer volume of people wanting a drink. Not Sarah. She never stopped, and never broke a sweat. It was little wonder she was head bar supervisor.

'You're a moron,' she said, matter of factly. A slightly inebriated man standing next to Rory raised his eyebrows, pointing to his chest. Or trying to anyway. It hit his shoulder instead. Sarah flashed him her best 'the customer is right' smile. 'No darling, not you. My friend here. Enjoy your night,' she added, effectively ending any conversation he might have attempted to start. 'You,' she repeated, jabbing her finger Rory's way with one hand and taking money with another. 'You're an idiot. Why do you insist on fawning over her, when she doesn't even remember your name half the time?'

Rory looked offended. 'She does so remember my name!'

Sarah gave him a despairing look. 'She calls you Ryan, Rory.'

'So?' Rory shrugged, glancing back in Sasha's direction longingly. 'She knows it starts with an R. It's not far off.'

Sarah shoved two glasses at once under the optics, passing them down the bar and lined up shot glasses. 'Rory, lots of things start with R. Like ridiculous, and rude.' She flicked her eyes to him, her features softening. 'And remote. Like your chances.'

Rory chuckled. 'You really don't like her, do you?'

Sarah raised her eyebrows at him, before she quickly placed the shots on a round tray and passed it to one of the shot girls. They were dressed like Easter bunnies tonight, in honour of the bank holiday weekend. Sexy bunnies, obviously. Cotton tails and skimpy outfits, not full on furry bodysuit and big teeth. Only the sluttiest and most sexist ideas will do for his father's events. The bar staff had bunny ears on too, in keeping with the theme. Sarah was not impressed, to say the least.

'Don't be mad,' he said coyly. 'It's making your ears twitch.' The look she gave him could shatter a chocolate egg at twenty paces.

'Don't get me started Rory, I warn you. And it's not that I don't like her, it's just that I don't like her for you. It doesn't fit.'

'Fit with what?' Rory asked, puzzled. The drunk man next to him looked equally confused and let out a loud burp to say as such. 'I think we would be a great couple.'

His friend smiled at him, and her eyes moved higher into her brunette hairline. He recognised the look on her face, he had seen her give it many a time to her daughter Annabelle. It was a look that you gave a child who had asked a difficult question.

'I know you think that, but I just don't see it Ror. I really think you'll get hurt.'

He shook his head. 'I won't get hurt, it's fine. I have a plan. She'll see me here all the time, and eventually we'll get to talking, and that's when we'll get together. Easy.'

Sarah looked like he had just told her he still believed in Santa. She pushed her bunny ears back into the centre of her head and nodded. 'Okay Rory, just remember, you are a nice guy. Some girls just don't want that.'

Rory had a flash of his mother's face, urging him to be better than his father. To be a good man. 'Why? Why wouldn't a woman want that?'

Sarah looked at him, and her expression changed when she realised he was being genuine. He really wanted to know. He really was a lovely guy, she wished he would see how perfect he was. She knew all about his mother, and the promise he had kept, but what his mother didn't tell him about was the women. Back then, even rom-coms always went with the underdog, the poorly paid genuine guy. The pimply geek won heart of fair maiden. Nowadays, women were told stories of the Magic Mikes, the Christian Greys. Attitude, aloofness and washboard abs, all put into packages of helicopter flying billionaires or plucky business men. Would Fitzwilliam Darcy have taken a paddleboard to the bottom of Elizabeth Bennett on their wedding night? One thinks not. She only had to look at her own love life to see that this was true. I mean, look who she had ended up with. The walking hard-on himself, complete with flash car, dangerous, exciting job, nice bottom in a pair of jeans, caveman attitude to women. The two men couldn't be more different. None of this helped Rory though, and she didn't have the heart to tell him either. She tried anyway. She had to protect him.

'Rory, in our teens and twenties, we watch a lot of films, read a lot of books - everyone wants a bad boy. We all want the motorbike riding, fast talking guy with all the cool moves. Women want excitement. Look at your dad! You're too nice for someone like Sasha. She'll probably go for someone who doesn't deserve to lick your boots. It's just how things are. We don't live in a rom-com Rory, nice guys finish last. Women, God love us, go for the douche bags, not the good ones.'

'Like you did?' He countered and wished he had bitten his tongue off. She ignored him, walking a little further down the bar and taking an order. He could tell by the sudden flush in her cheeks and the look on her face that his comment had stung. Bugger. Rory turned away from the bar, running his hands through his hair in frustration. Sasha was nowhere to be seen, and now he was stood with a drunk stranger at the end of a bar, probably looking every inch the saddo he felt. He finished off the bottle of water and left it on the bar. He headed for the back rooms, through the throng. He might as well get some work done while he was here. Going home to an empty house and eating leftovers from the fridge in front of Bear Grylls didn't really appeal. Plus, he did that last night.

He came to the toilet doors and swung a left, stopping in front of a door marked PRIVATE and tapping a code into the entry pad. As soon as he closed the door, the music from the club faded, and he walked down the long corridor towards the main office at the end. The locker room and staff room were empty, with everyone working on the floor. It was mercifully quiet, but Rory could hear a woman giggle as he got closer to the door. It was answered by a deep voice, and Rory cringed inwardly. His dad was obviously at work. He knocked on the office door loudly and was pleased when he heard a startled squeak and a series of rustling noises. He just hoped nothing had happened on his desk. Like last time. He knocked again, entering just as a blonde was putting on her heels and attempting to tame her nest of wild hair.

'Son!' His dad exclaimed, walked hurriedly from behind his own desk to greet him. He held out his hand offering a handshake, but Rory just looked at it, his lip curling in obvious disgust. Doug looked down at his hand and wiped it on his suit trousers, taking a step back. The blonde gave Rory the once over. Obviously finding him lacking at the side of his father, she gave them both a weak smile and with a wave of her long neon nails, she click-clacked out of the office. Rory looked at the door, and back at his dad before walking over to his desk and switching on his computer.

'So, working on a Friday night again?' Doug tried, walking across the shiny black tiled floor to the drinks cabinet. 'Drink?'

Rory logged in and glanced across at him. 'No thanks, I'm driving.'

Doug waved him away. 'I can get Mickey to drop you off. I'll be here late tonight anyway. '

Rory sighed, nodding slowly. 'I'll have one, but I can get a lift with Sarah. She has an early finish tonight.'

Doug's grin dimmed a little, but he soon recovered, setting to work on making their drinks. 'So, how's the love life?' He asked, and Rory resisted the urge to groan, both at the question and at his father's attempts at conversation. The man had just been caught having sex by his son, yet he still felt parental enough to enquire about his romantic life. Or lack of it. He was trying though, as awkwardly as always. He recognised that and threw his father a lifeline.

'Not much to report, Dad. Are these all the receipts you have?' He gestured to the spike on his desk, where a mess of paper had been speared onto it.

'What about Sarah? Still nothing? Er, yes…for now. I have more back at home, I can bring them in.' His dad walked to the space between the desks where a red leather couch was installed and sat down with his Scotch. The ice tinkled in the glass as he rested it on the arm rest and dropped his head against the back.

'Sarah?' Rory shook his head. 'No, Dad, we're best friends, you know that. She's like my sister. Besides, Greg's trying to prove himself.'

Doug snorted, curling his lip. 'Greg? That boy is bad news.

She can do better. Hell, half the pond weed in here are better than Greg.'

'Hey, that pond weed is Annabelle's dad, and Sarah's a smart woman. She's knows what he's doing.'

Doug rubbed at his face, draining the rest of his drink and going to refill it. 'I know, I knew the minute you brought her to me that she would do well here. I wouldn't be without her.'

'Yeah, plus it's a bonus having a bar manager you know won't sleep with you. The last one really screwed with the books.'

Doug raised his hands as if in surrender. 'Yes, yes, I know. I learnt my lesson, don't sleep with the management.'

'Or the staff at all would be nice,' Rory chided. 'Who was the blonde?'

'Drinks rep,' Doug said sheepishly. 'They want us to stock their new brand of shots. She left some samples. Will you ask Sarah to have a look?'

Rory nodded. 'I will, later. She's not really my biggest fan at the moment.' His dad grinned. 'Women, eh?'

Rory didn't answer, choosing instead to focus on the numbers. Maths soothed him. They followed a pattern, they understood him, and more importantly, he understood them.

CHAPTER THREE

Saturday

It was after midnight when Sarah's battered green Corsa turned into Rory's street. Sarah had pretty much ignored him since their earlier disagreement, and he had been about to hail a cab when she had come out of the club and started walking to the car park. Rory had walked with her automatically, making sure she got to her car safely, but she had motioned for him to get in. The car was a bit of a junker, the back seat littered with Annabel's Lego and science fact books. It had a dent in the front passenger side, where Sarah had scraped it coming down Rory's drive one particularly stressful afternoon, and a slight remnant of a scratch down the driver door where some overzealous groupie of Doug's had mistaken Sarah for his latest squeeze and attacked it with her heel. Doug had offered to pay of course, even to replace the car, but Sarah wouldn't hear of it, choosing to cover it herself. When she dug her heels in, it was best to just leave it. Rory really admired that in her, even though it was frustrating at times. She had been the same since they were kids. He wished he could be more like that himself sometimes. Sarah always spoke her mind too, apart from with Greg. Rory kept it all in, sometimes having imaginary arguments with himself later at home, saying the things he wanted to say at the time, to that person. Not healthy, but there it was.

Sarah pulled up outside his house and turned off the engine. The car chugged to a spluttering stop.

'Thanks for the lift. You working tomorrow?'

'Yep, if I can get a minute I have to study too. I have a paper due, so I am hoping to get a few hours in before my shift. Annabel is dead set on finishing her science project ahead of time though, so it's doubtful.'

Rory chuckled. 'What did she decide on in the end?'

Sarah smiled, rolling her eyes and Rory realised she wasn't mad anymore. Annabel had that effect on people. 'She's decided to plot the time line on global warming. She is focusing on the fact that Earth Hour is not taken up by the general population. She was up late last night making identical globes. She wants to go to the toy shop too tomorrow.'

'She actually wants to go toy shopping? For an actual new toy?' He looked shocked, and Sarah tittered.

'No, of course not. She wants to buy some wooden toy animals, to show the effect on wildlife around the world. Mum's not impressed, she has her craft group coming round on Sunday, and the dining room table is littered with papier mache and balloons. She keeps dropping hints, but Annabel tells her Operation Save the World is more important than a silly craft group. My mum is furious. They are so alike - it's like having two children to look after. I swear, I'm so glad I'm training to teach adults, not children. I'd go gaga.'

'No paid teaching hours yet?'

Sarah shook her head. 'With everything else, I can't commit to the hours they want. Volunteering is okay for now. I get my placements signed off. Hopefully once I qualify, I can get something very part time, work my way up when Annabel is older.'

'Why don't I take Annabel to the toy shop in the morning, give you chance to study? Then you can get the project done and off the table for your mum's group.'

Sarah was already shaking her head no. 'I can't ask you to do that-'

Rory cut her off. 'Sar, you didn't ask me, and I am her godfather. It's in the contract, free babysitting. Come on, let me help. I would only be hanging around the house anyway.'

Sarah smiled and kissed him on the cheek, pulling him into a tight hug. 'Rory, thanks - that's amazing. I am so stressed at the moment, you wouldn't believe.'

Rory nodded. He knew just how hard Sarah worked, and once again he wanted to give Greg the deadbeat dad a piece of his mind. He said nothing though, hugging her back. He never said anything.

***

Saturday morning, and the bank holiday shopping crowd was out in force, searching for bargains. Kids hyped up on sugar from their hoards annoyed parents left and right, and retail workers could be heard collectively sighing and wishing they were laid on the sofa watching Ben Hur. Rory was walking arm in arm with a gorgeous girl on his arm. As they walked around the town of Leeds, he could see passers by looking at her, even turning their heads as they walked along the street.

'Are you really going to wear that all day?' He asked, a slight smirk on his face as he looked down at his companion. Annabel looked up and even behind the surgeon's mask, he could see her roll her eyes.

'Uncle Roar-Roar, do you know how many germ microbes the average child carries? Just in their bodies alone - then they go touching everyone and coughing and sneezing everywhere. Eugh, I'll have to disinfect the props we buy before I can even touch them for my project. I can't get sick, I have too much to do!' Her voice was muffled under the mask, and Rory resisted the compulsion to laugh by quickly glancing into the nearest shop window. He locked eyes with Sasha Birkenstock, who was sat having her nails done in the up market salon they were standing in front of. He went to wave, but she had already looked away, no hint of recognition on her face.

'Who are you waving at?' Annabel asked, pushing her mask clad nose closer to the window. Rory steered her away back towards the toy shop.

'No-one, Brains,' he said sadly. 'Just someone from work. She didn't see me.'

'Is she your girl friend or your girlfriend? Mum told me the difference the other day.'

'No, nothing like that. She's more of a work friend.' Worse luck, he added silently.

'I am so not having a boyfriend yet. If I am going to be top of my class again this year, I need to focus on my goals, not on silly boys.'

Rory laughed as he navigated his charge through the early morning shoppers. She was so her mother's daughter in many ways.

'Daddy came round this morning. Mummy was trying to study, so he didn't stay long.' And not in others, he added in his head. Sarah needed to be tougher about the boys in her life. She wasn't even in a relationship with him anymore, but he still hung around her like a bad smell. Eau de dickwad.

'Oh yeah? Did you not want him to take you to the toy shop?'

He looked at her sweet face, and he could tell she was wrinkling her nose under the mask.

'No, he just came to borrow some money again from Mummy. I didn't tell him about the toy shop. I didn't want him to come.'

Rory clenched his jaw, picturing Greg being on their shopping trip. Not a good idea, with so many plate glass shop windows just nearby. 'Oh yeah, well, I am rather excellent company.' He pulled a funny face at her, pushing his lips out into a pout and crossing his eyes. Annabel giggled.

'Exactly! I told Mummy not to tell him, he just gets mad.'

Rory knew exactly what she was talking about. Greg wasn't the most relaxed person on the planet. He squeezed her hand gently, and she squeezed his back.

'Let's go buy some toys!' he said loudly, making a lady with a shopping bag nearby jump in surprise.

Annabel groaned through the mask. 'For the last time, they're props!'

They entered the shop and Annabel gripped the mask tighter to her face with one hand and Rory to her with the other. To be fair, the sight was something to behold. Kids of every shape and size crowded the aisles, looking through shelves of pinks and blues with harassed looking adults. A young boy wearing a t-shirt saying 'Mummy's little angel' came screaming past them with an action figure in his hand, his mother running after him.

'Georgie, put it back NOW! One...two...don't make me count to three!'

'Eugh, and so sexist. I knew it. When will they stop gender stereotyping?' Annabel snorted. She grabbed Rory's hand and pulled him along with her. 'According to my Google Earth Maps search, the wooden animals I want are near the tills. Let's go, Roar-Roar!' He let himself be pulled along, half expecting her to start sanitising children with the anti-bac gel she had insisted on bringing. Still, Uncle Roar Roar was happy to go into battle for his little Brains. Annabel was one female he did understand. The depressing fact that a schoolgirl was the only willing female company he had these days was not lost on him. He needed to come up with a plan, and soon. Either that or buy a cat.

'What do you want these wooden animals for, anyway? To stick to your globes, showing where they live?'

'Yes,' Annabel nodded innocently, looking through the rack. 'And on the truthful one, I am going to cut them up, showing how they will die unless mankind changes their selfish ways.' She picked up a wooden elephant, looking at its carved long tusks.

'See?' she said, smiling sweetly. 'These tusks will snap right off, symbolising the barbaric ivory trade.'

A father stood next to Rory stood open mouthed, looking in horror at them both. The child in the pram he was pushing was sat eating his own bogey. Rory smiled proudly and leaned over.

'She gets it from her mother.'

***

Sunday

Rory woke to the drip drip drip of the tap in the en suite. First world problem, he realised, but still, it drove him mad. It had pervaded his dreams the night before, although the tapping had morphed into Sasha, dancing on the bar in a hot pink dress whilst Gary Barlow sang and played the piano. When his alarm had chimed at 7am, he had fully expected to open his eyes to see Sasha, or even Gary in his bed. Thankfully, when he finally prised open a peeper, his checked blue pillow was empty. As usual. Rolling onto his back, he stared up at the ceiling, listening to that damn tap mocking him. Drip. Single. Drip. All alone. Drip drip. Undateable loner. Quite a judgemental thing, that tap. Smug metal git. It was okay for him, taps hung out in pairs usually. The legwork was done. All plumbed up and matched. Bish bash bosh. No worrying about meeting the one, finding someone to share their life with. Easy. Rory groaned. He was that fed up this morning that he was jealous of a faucet. It would be funny if it weren't so darn tragic. He thought back to seeing Sasha in the salon, of her laughing and joking with the other customers as she got her nails done.

He wondered what kind of plans she had for the day. No doubt something spectacular. Fancy breakfast with someone dashing, Instagram worthy avocados and eggs Benedict on some sunny terrace, followed by an afternoon of PR work and brand promotion. Her Saturday evenings were either spent at the club or out in some flash place, photos of celebs and passion fruit cocktails. He knew this because the club's Instagram account followed her company, since the two often worked together on events in Leeds. Rory wasn't even on Instagram. What would be the point? His firm was accountancy. What was he going to photograph, Gill's Star Wars figures? A calculator at a jaunty angle on his desk? He couldn't even think about the comments that would produce.

Hauling himself out from under his crisp clean sheets, he padded barefoot to the bathroom and looked at the offending enemy. The bathroom was pristine as usual, his toiletries all lined up on the glass shelves above the basin.

The tap seemed to be getting worse, and Rory didn't relish the thought of spending another night lying in bed listening to the same noise. He already knew he wouldn't be able to sleep. Besides, what else was he going to do with his Sunday? He didn't frequent the gym, he didn't go to church, and he didn't watch sport. What did people do with their free time nowadays? Rory was beginning to hate Sundays with a passion, even detest them rolling around at the end of each week. People usually saw Monday as the worst day of the week, but not him. Monday meant work, lunch with Sarah, routine. Hearing about Gill's conventions and box set sessions watching Star Trek, or whatever other science fiction obsession he had moved onto. It was what he usually looked forward to, but the further time went on, the more unsatisfied with his lot he felt. Of course, he had dinner with his father later, but that often failed to improve his mood any. God knows which MENSA candidate would be attempting to cook something edible this week. A couple of months ago, Rory had spent his Sunday evening and most of Monday hugging the toilet for dear life, whilst ejecting his bodily fluids from every outlet he possessed. Sarah had wanted to take him to hospital, but he was just too embarrassed to let anyone else see him. She had ended up sleeping in his bed close by whilst he laid on the bathroom floor, moaning and shivering. He would never again eat beef casserole, and his dad had soon parted ways with little Miss Masterchef. His dad hadn't mentioned anything this week, so perhaps they would be able to fend for themselves for once.

Rory sighed and made a decision. He would do something that other people did on a Sunday. He would fix the damn tap. If you can't beat them, DIY.

Forty minutes later, he pulled his brown Volvo 740 into the car park of the retail shopping centre and looked out at the crowds of people milling around from shop to shop. It had to be said, the majority of the people didn't look best pleased to be there. Armed with the knowledge he had gleaned from a Google search, he headed for the plumbing supplies. He located the washers on one side of an aisle boasting an array of baffling pipes, rubber rings and other scary odds and sods that Rory didn't recognise the name of. Locating the rows of washers, he was none the wiser. He had expected one brand and one size, but he soon realised that this had been a little naive. Giving up, he went off to find an apron clad assistant. He found one who was just returning from helping a woman put a stack of grow bags into her car.

'Excuse me, do you have a minute?'

The man, who was quite buff under his shirt, smiled politely. 'Yes Sir, what are you looking for?'

Rory started to walk back to the aisle, the man following. 'I need a new washer, my bathroom tap is driving me mad.'

The man nodded. 'Missus sent you, did she?'

Rory shook his head. 'Nope, not married.' Why was that even a question?

'Ah,' he said, tapping the side of his rather red nose. 'Impressing the girlfriend, I get ya. What size?'

Rory shrugged, giving the girlfriend comment a wide swerve. 'I'm not sure to be honest.'

'Okay, you brought the old washer?'

Rory frowned. 'Er no, it's still in the tap.'

The man shrugged again. 'Ok, what's the tap?'

Rory pulled his phone from his pocket, flicking up a photo and showing it to the man. 'That one,' he said, confidently. The man looked at him as though he had just showed him a nude picture.

'Er, I can't really tell what brand of tap that is, or the washer size. I don't think we stock them. Do you want to come back?'

The man didn't say 'with a grown up' out loud, but Rory could practically hear his thoughts, and cringed inwardly. How was it that even as an adult, other adults somehow feel more adult like? Rory felt as though he was still wearing braces and talking awkwardly to his woodwork teacher.

'Ah, sure yes, thanks.' He smiled and nodded, before making a swift escape down another aisle. He headed to the main doors, trying to dislodge the flashing neon sign above his head that said DIY VIRGIN. He felt like he had left his man card at home. Or never got it in the first place. He pulled out his phone.

'Gill?' he said to the answering voice. 'You know a handyman?'

CHAPTER FOUR

Sarah woke to the sound of hushed laughter from downstairs and smiled. Annabel and Bunny would be downstairs now, making their traditional funny face pancakes. They did this every Sunday, letting her sleep in. Another thing to feel guilty for…the fact that she was sleeping, instead of actually being present and making pancakes with her daughter. She groaned and rolled over. Her feet still pulsed from walking up and down the bar all night, and she felt like she had a hangover, though as usual, she had been as sober as a judge, watching other people have fun and live their lives. She was always a spectator, on the outside looking in at others out there, doing their thing. She kept telling herself that things would get easier once she qualified as a fully fledged adult tutor, but she knew that she had to get there first. Even then she could only work part time days, trying to avoid childcare costs and stay awake long enough to teach a class. In the meantime, her daughter grew bigger every day, and she didn't get the time to spend with her. Time she would never get back.

Thumping the pillowcase beside her in frustration, she looked at the clock. Nine am. By the time she crawled into bed last night, it was gone five o'clock, and then Greg had phoned at half past to try and cadge a lift home from whatever skanky hole he had crawled out of. She hadn't answered, putting it on silent instead. No doubt he wouldn't bother showing up to see Annabel either. Probably say he bagged an extra shift. The guy was a walking contradiction, but he never allowed himself to be called on his crap. Everyone else messed up, never him of course. She thought back to the early days when the goggles of romance and lust blinded her to his many faults. She was the original cliché - hopeless romantic girl falls for the dashing fire fighter.

Who didn't love a six foot two, blonde haired, blue eyed fireman with guns of steel? He even got the odd wandering look from the grandmas as he rescued their kittens. (Yes, this does happen. Quite often, especially since he was transferred to Leeds Fire Station.) They had met on a night out, him fresh from fire school, her celebrating finishing her degree with Rory and the other students. There he was, surrounded by other walls of sturdy knicker dropping flesh, downing pints like they were thimbles of water, and thoroughly making a show of themselves in Miranda's. Rory didn't approve of course and tried to steer her away. She should have let him, she normally did. Alas, beer goggles and post study stress release won, and pretty soon she was being twirled around the dance floor by the Yorkshire equivalent of Alexander Skarsgard. Of course, he turned out to be more like Eric Northman in terms of being a complete alpha male arsehole. By the time the rose-tinted glasses fell off, she was stuffed. Pregnant and unable to rely on the father for anything other than being a complete and utter liability. Fast forward seven years, and she was still here. Still tied to him, and still in some kind of twisted baby-mama relationship. She was expecting a sister wife any day now. To be fair, if she was any good at babysitting, it would be a bonus at this point in her life.

Looking at her phone, she saw that Rory had sent her a

message. She smiled as she read his text, telling her about his foray into DIY. Rory was a lot of things, but handy with a spanner was not one of the first things that sprang to mind. She clicked the call button to ring him, but at the last second Greg's face popped up on the screen and she answered it before she could stop herself.

'Er, sorry, I thought you would be still asleep babe. Sat on the phone, were you?'

She rolled her eyes. Years ago, he would have been checking her phone, seeing if she was talking to anyone. She always knew he did it, she had even started being a bit secretive with it while he was around. Even now, when he had no right and she had nothing to hide anyway, she still kept her phone in sight when he came to the house. She knew it wound him up, but she just couldn't help it. There was never anything on it anyway, just friends from uni and work, and he had already made sure to 'vet' those people, asking questions. She called him out on it all the time, but he just played the Annabel card. 'I have a right to know just who is in my daughter's life, Sarah. It's called parenting.'

It was pathetic, and unfounded, but that was Greg. It didn't matter that he was probably out doing anything that looked half decent in a skirt, or that they weren't even sleeping together. Sarah might be trapped, but she wasn't daft. That part of their relationship was over long ago, but they still kept up the charade of happy caring co-parents for Annabel's sake. Sarah figured life would change once their daughter grew up, and their ties were loosened year on year. She longed for the day when they only had to endure each other at unavoidable family occasions. Bunny would never stop reminding her though, that by that time she would be older.

'Older, wrinkled, and still alone! Do you think he won't have some dolly bird on his arm at your only child's wedding? You can bet the farm he will, and who will you take? Me? That will look super great won't it, two single old bags together!'

Sarah always laughed off her concerns, but the reality was that this was probably her future. Her brilliant clever daughter would grow up, move out and set the world alight, and she would be here. Still living with her mother. Single, skint and dried up. Till her mother passed, of course. Then she would be utterly alone, sobbing into her denture cream while Greg carried on like Hugh Hefner.

'Babe, you fallen back to sleep?' Greg's voice snapped her back from her Miss Havisham nightmare.

'No, I'm here. Don't call me babe either. I just got up Greg. What time are you coming to pick up Annabel?'

He had started erm-ing and arr-ing before she had even finished the question. 'That's just it, I can't have her till later, I have something on.'

'What do you have on?' She asked quickly. 'Work emergency? Car trouble? Oh no, it was car trouble last week, work emergency the week before.'

There was a pause on the line before Greg answered. His tone told her that he was not amused about being questioned. 'I'm just busy, Sarah. I do have a life you know. I'll take her out for tea about five o'clock.'

Sarah huffed down the phone but said nothing. If she picked a fight, he wouldn't come at all, and Annabel needed a father. Sarah knew what it was like to grow up without one, and even Greg was better than just a photo on the wall. Thank God she had been wise enough to never live with him, it had made ending things much easier when she had wised up for real. Annabel had never had to go through the pain of her parents breaking up, though she had to convince herself most days that their situation was normal.

'Fine, I'm in work at eight o'clock, so have her back by then, so we can get her to bed on time. I don't want to leave it all to Mum.'

'Great, see you then. Kiss to the doodlebug from me.' He clicked the line off with a smarmy goodbye.

Sarah glared at the phone, suddenly wishing she had never got up.

***

The plumber was just finishing up, and Rory couldn't wait for him to leave. He had had quite enough emasculation for one day, and he had already resolved to either hire a regular, non judgemental handyman for these things or just move house next time something went kaput. The arse crack was all ego and was still chuckling to himself as he brought his tool bag bumping down the stairs.

'So,' he said, pulling up ineffectually on his jeans, 'with callout and parts, it's £125.50. The good news is, the washer was only 50p!' He guffawed, slapping his thigh with a meaty hand. Rory nodded, smiling as he pulled out his wallet. Smug git. The bars of Sex on Fire rang out, and the guy held up his finger, turning away down the hallway. Rory pulled his phone out of his own pocket. No messages. Sarah hadn't replied, but she would no doubt still be asleep, or wrangling with Greg about him coming to pick up Annabel. He would ask her to go for a coffee later, try to salvage the dire day.

'I know, baby,' Rory heard him say. 'I'm on my way now, I just have one more job to call at and then I'm there, okay?' Rory could hear a woman's silky tones dripping down the phone. 'Oooh, you naughty girl, you wait till I get my hands on you. Ah bugger, my call waiting's going off. It might be a job, see you soon.' He clicked off the call, pressing a button on the handset. He spotted Rory stood there, wallet in hand and winked at him.

'Angie, baby! I've been waiting all day to hear your sexy voice. Tonight? Yeah sure, I have a few jobs on this aft though, will eight o'clock do?'

Rory watched open mouthed as he proceeded to thrust at the hall end table, all the while simpering on the phone to the woman who was making goo-goo noises down the phone. She rang off, and the man air punched vigorously.

'That my son, is how you do it!' He pulled once more at his jeans, but the instant his hands left his waistband, they slumped back down.

'Cheers, do you need a receipt?' The man didn't look as though he even had a receipt book, and he stared at Rory as though daring him to say yes. Rory just wanted to get the lothario out of his house and he shook his head. The accountant in him wanted to audit the hell out of this slimebag.

'No, that's fine. Thanks for coming out on a Sunday.'

The man grinned. 'No worries, Sundays are always a bit tricky on the woman front, if you know what I mean. I call it my juggling day, so getting called out is a pretty sweet gig.'

Rory nodded, willing his lip not to curl up in disgust. How did this guy get all the women?

'So, how do you get all these women?' The words had jumped from his thought process straight onto his tongue, and out of his now open mouth. The man grinned wolfishly.

'Mate, the women love a man who can work with his hands, a strong bloke who treats 'em mean. You flash your guns and a bit of chat at a girl and she'll be putty in your hands.'

'That's it? What about romance and wining and dining?'

He guffawed. 'Mate, you still have to do that now and then, keep 'em sweet, but you want to keep them on their toes too. No woman likes Mr SAD.' He counted on three fingers. 'Safe and dependable, get it? S-A-D. No lass lies in bed on a night dreaming about a man who is gonna come along and clean the toilet and balance their cheque book. Nah, they dream about the bad boys, the men who pick them up and sweep them off their feet. The men that keep their interest going and their knickers flapping.'

Rory frowned, but oddly it made sense. He thought of Sarah's comment about nice guys. Sasha had never looked twice at him, even though they crossed paths all the time. He saw what type of men she seemed to take notice of though. The larger than life, confident types. Maybe this knuckle headed insult to feminism did have a point. After all, his own dad was a living example. He never whispered sweet nothings, yet his bedroom needed a revolving door when Rory was growing up.

'Trust me mate,' he said, whipping the cash out of Rory's hand with one hand, whilst reaching for his tool bag with the other. 'It works, me and the lads have them eating out of the palm of our hands. What do you do for a living?' He looked around the house as if noticing it for the first time. 'Pretty nice pad, big for just you. You a suit?'

Rory nodded. 'I have an accountancy firm with a friend, yes.'

'Ah,' the man said, slapping Rory on the shoulder with such force it almost spun him like a top. 'A number cruncher eh? Not working with the ladies, is it? Not one to flash the cash, are you?' He looked around pointedly at the decor. Glancing around himself, he did have to admit, it had the faint whiff of single man forlorn about it. It was nice, but not very inviting, homely. Maybe he should rethink his strategy, or lack thereof.

'Well, I am single actually, yes.' The man grinned at him, as if to say, 'I told you so'.

'But you like women, yeah?' Rory looked down at his cardigan and slippers momentarily before answering.

'Yes, I like women. Well, one woman in particular actually.'

The man reached for the door handle, standing in the doorway. The sun was shining outside. Rory thought how nice it would be to sit outside the coffee shop later, drinking coffee and reading the Sunday papers with Sarah. Maybe Annabel and Bunny would come too if Greg was too hungover to be bothered with his daughter today.

'Well mate, listen to me. No cardigan or accountant ever won fair maiden without a bit of a game plan. Can't you just tell her you work in banking? Women love those banker wankers, Wolf of Wall Street and all that. Jazz yourself up a bit, start calling the shots, and you'll have 'em lining up.'

He started to walk down the garden path, whistling to himself. Rory stood staring after him. He shoved his tools into the back of his van and saluted him before stepping into the driver's seat. Winding the window down, he looked across at Rory one more time before starting the engine.

'Mate, you need to get rid of the gigs too. Lois Lane didn't fancy Clark Kent, did she? Nah, she wanted Superman. The glasses and cardi combo need to do one!'

He flicked on his music, laughing as he drove away to the boom boom of his music. No doubt he was off to see one of his conquests. Rory didn't know whether to feel violated or impressed. The man had a point though. He closed his front door and turning to go to the kitchen, he caught sight of himself in the hall mirror. He did have a look of Clark Kent, Christopher Reeves era. He took off his glasses, squinting at himself. His hair was cut a bit severely too, very short back and sides. His dark brown hair and brown eyes made him look a little pale, washed out now you could see more of his face. Perhaps he should rethink his look. He resolved to go into Leeds on his lunch break tomorrow, see what he could fathom out in the shops. His gaze fell to a framed picture of his mother. She was holding him in her arms, both of them laughing and smiling into the camera lens. It was from their last holiday together, sat on the beach in Greece without a care in the world. Before she got sick, and before Dad fell apart altogether on the parenting front.

'I haven't forgotten what you said Mum, but things need to change.' He looked around his neat house one more time, finding it rather sparse and lacking now, and headed off to make a spot of lunch before trying Sarah again.

CHAPTER FIVE

It was just coming up to teatime, and the weather was still beautiful. The air was filled with warmth, and the gentle breeze that caressed them as they sat outside their favourite coffee shop took the sting of the heat from their skin. Annabel was with Greg, but Sarah was frazzled by the handover.

'He still turned up late, can you believe that? I agreed to him coming for her at five, and he swans up at half past stinking of perfume. I bet he'll bring her back late too, and then she'll be exhausted for school tomorrow. He knows I'm working tonight and have college tomorrow as well. I swear Rory, I could cheerfully murder him!'

Rory shook his head. 'I already told you, tell him to be on time or not bother at all. It's not fair on Belle.'

The only person in the whole world that was allowed to call her daughter Belle wasn't either of Annabel's parents, or her grandmother, who she loved dearly. No, it was Uncle Roar-Roar, who she absolutely thought the world of. The name had come from Beauty and the Beast, a name from a story Sarah had loved since her dear departed dad had read it to her. The idea of a girl having her own library and falling in love with a prince sounded pretty perfect to Sarah, who loathed her own rather boring name. Annabel - of course - hated it. She didn't want to be married to a prince, she wanted to cure cancer, conquer space and only go out with a man who was just like

Uncle Roar-Roar.

Rory had always called her Belle, from the moment he saw her born, and she had never minded, but as soon as she was old enough to speak, she would get especially cross with anyone else who shortened her name in that manner. Rory found it amusing, Sarah thought it was adorable, Greg detested it and tried to call her it all the time. She never let him, of course, and would even pretend not to hear him when he called. This only annoyed him further, so he started calling her his doodlebug. A pet name between the two. Sarah knew it was only to compete with Rory, who didn't engage with Greg or his petty games. Annabel tolerated his moods, and the annoying nickname, to keep the peace. Even at the tender age of six, she knew which battles to pick, and how to play a man. Sarah just wished her own choices had been wiser, but she could never imagine not having Annabel now, despite her father.

'I do tell him Ror, I tell him all the time, but the amount of soot and ash between those ears makes it impossible to penetrate his brain. He was out last night again, he thinks I'm stupid. He forgets he dials me up like a taxi when he's drunk, not that I ever go. He will have had some fancy piece fawning all over him and making him a Sunday roast, while his daughter has to sit in all day and wait for him to remember she exists.'

Rory pursed his lips but said nothing. Greg reminded him of his own father at times, and the urge to intervene always prickled at his nerve endings. He would love to tell the slimy piece of work just what he thought about him, but of course, that wasn't his style. Truth was, Greg would be more likely to receive a strongly worded complaint letter than a good bop on the chin.

'So, what did you do today?' He asked, trying to change the subject. The waitress brought a tray filled with coffee and toasted sandwiches, and the pair smiled at her warmly before setting to work on them.

'I worked for most of it, lesson planning mostly, and made notes on an assignment for college. It's due in 3 weeks but I need to get it in before the holidays really, or Annabel will have to talk to the back of my head as usual.' She pulled apart a cheese and ham toastie, the cheese dripping down onto the plate in a long string. She folded a napkin around it and put it to her lips, groaning as the food touched her taste buds.

'You're a good mum, Belle knows that. Stop beating yourself up all the time! Can't you cut your hours at the club? I can ask Dad for a raise if you like. He can afford to pay you more, you know.'

Sarah shook her head, a mouthful of cheesy bread. 'No way, I need every penny at the moment. Mum's savings are for her retirement, I don't want her dipping in to pay for the pair of us. I think she would have retired earlier if it hadn't been for me. The house is paid for, and she has a decent payout from Dad's death benefits. I don't want her going back to work when she could be enjoying herself. Your dad already pays me a good whack, and I turned down a raise last week.' She took a slurp of her coffee.

'Why on earth did you do that?' he asked, exasperated. 'You need the money!'

Sarah rolled her eyes. 'Ror, I know I'm already on more than the going rate for a bar supervisor. The raise was too much. I'm not a charity case, and it's not like he was asking me to do any extra work for it. I know he did it to be kind, but I want to pay my way.'

Rory scowled, taking a sip of his own much needed caffeine hit. 'You should have taken it, for Belle at least. He can afford it.'

Sarah shrugged. 'Yes, he can, but it doesn't mean he should just give his money away. He pays me well, you can't knock him for how he treats his staff.'

Rory raised a dark brow and she laughed.

'Okay, okay, some things you can knock, but not his pay rates. Besides, he's never tried it on with me.' Rory's lip curled in obvious horror.

'Eugh. I should hope so too! I would bloody kill him!'

Sarah sat back in her chair and watched her best friend disembowel a toastie with a knife, his face scrunched up behind his black rimmed glasses. He was wearing brown loafers, cream slacks, white shirt and blue tie. It was all topped off with a thin cream cardigan. He looked so dapper, at odds somewhat with the other coffee shop Sunday crowd, who were all jeans and jeggings. She herself had on a cornflower blue summer dress and low- slung silver sandals. They looked like a couple, it struck her for a second.

'So,' she said, shaking away the odd notion. 'Did you get your plumbing fixed?'

The groan he released from the pit of his stomach got the other customers, and one startled passer-by carrying a guitar looking his way.

'The man was gross. He basically made me feel like a complete idiot, and then juggled women on the phone like they were some kind of sexy bean bags. I swear, I'm doing it wrong.'

'Mate, not everyone is good at DIY.'

'You are!' he said, pointing a slender finger at her. 'At

university, everyone rang you in the dorms for help. You even plastered Belle's room!'

'I had to!' She giggled. 'I can't afford to hire a handyman and you get pretty handy with no dad around.'

Rory pursed his lips, and Sarah thought how cute he looked. He always did it when he was processing his thoughts, and she sat in companionable silence, waiting for him to speak.

'I had a dad around, but he never taught me those things. Instead, I learnt to cook and bake and sew. I can make a mean casserole and sew my own buttons back on, but not fix a leaky tap! What woman is going to want to settle down with that? The plumber was fighting them off, and he was more like Dad than me.' He rested his chin on his fingers, tapping his index digit on his lips. He left a slight sheen on them from the melted cheese. 'Maybe that's what I need to do Sar, start changing how I do the whole dating thing. Start the whole dating thing, actually.'

She leaned forward and gripping his chin lightly between her own fingers, she wiped at the grease on his lips. He didn't flinch, just stared at her with his big brown eyes. 'What do you think, worth a shot?' She didn't say anything at first, wanting to tell him never to change, that a woman would come along who would see him for the man he was, but his hopeful eyes stopped her. She knew he wasn't happy being alone, and he deserved some happiness. He always looked out for everyone else, it was about time someone had his back for once.

'Talk to Gill, see what he thinks, but I think that if it's really what you want, go for it,' she said, wiping her own hands on the napkin and reaching down by her chair for her handbag. She pulled out her purse, and her notepad fell out. As she went to pick it up, she saw pictures that had been drawn by Belle on the blank pages. Most of them were stick people, three or four in each one. She looked at them smiling, till she realised that the three people were her, Belle and Rory. Some were with her grandmother, Bunny, too. As she looked through quickly, she saw Greg wasn't even in it. One even had Doug in, smiling at Bunny. The poor girl had literally drawn her father out of her life.

'I tell you what,' she said, willing her flushed cheeks to calm down. 'I'll not only support you, I'll bloody well join you. I need to get back out there too.'

Rory's brows hit his hairline as he looked at her in shock. 'What about Greg?'

Sarah shook her head. 'I will never ever get back with that man.'

Rory looked sick at the prospect. 'No, of course not! I just meant how will he take you dating again? You've stayed single so far. Doesn't he just think you're on a break?'

'I couldn't give a rat's ass what he thinks. I'm sick of telling him it's not going to happen. He sticks his hose into any girl he wants, and might I add he did this when we were together.' She motioned to the waitress to refill her coffee cup.

Rory said nothing, just nodding. The waitress came and filled both their cups, smiling at them both.

CHAPTER SIX

Gill Cohen stood in the toilets of Leeds Arena and wiggled the iris of his eye back into place. The ice blue contact lenses he was wearing felt dry against his eyeballs, the effects of the anxiety he was feeling mixed with the air conditioning whizzing around the different stalls and exhibits. His costume was amazing, and he had felt amazing that morning, getting up and dressing, heading to the arena for the latest Cosplay event. He knew that his costume would definitely cause an impact, but as usual he had underestimated one thing. Well, one person, more than a thing. That person was Jon Snow. King of the Nights Watch, illegitimate Stark child, flash bearded pretty boy in a fur coat Jon Snow. Gill hated him with a passion. Or he did after today anyway. Today was the Cosplay competition for Game of Thrones, and Gill had been waiting for months to show off his costume. He had made it himself and it was pretty epic. He had been excited as he was as a boy, when one birthday he went dressed as He-Man. Everyone loved it, and he was the star of the show amongst the other children. He had felt that way again this morning, walking into the arena with the white walker costume on, looking through his ice blue contact lenses at the people who stopped and turned to look at his geeky awesomeness. Then he saw her, and his heart flipped. She was wearing a blonde wig, long and curled down her back covering her own brunette ringlets. She was dressed in a cream floaty gown, the train kissing the carpeted floor as she stood, head back laughing.

He felt that familiar tingle in his ice-cold walker heart as he strode across the stadium towards her. He imagined what he would look like; confident, turning heads his way, all the while training his eyes on her. Zeroing in on her like a raven would on its target, spying for a worg. She would turn any moment, and the laughter in her throat would turn to unbridled lust. She would move away from the crowd, transfixed on him, his very own Khaleesi. She would move away from the crowd she was immersed in, suddenly not caring who she left behind, because there was only him. Her perfect other half. He would stride over purposefully, lift her into his arms, her long sleeves draping down his manly leather clad shoulders, and then he would kiss her...

It was then he saw what Dinah, said object of romantic montage, was laughing at. Eric Dimplewell. Eric Dimplewell, dressed as Jon Snow. Gill was so taken aback that he stumbled a little in his stride, and an elderly lady wearing a dragon costume propped him up by his elbow.

'You alright, duck? You look a bit pale!' She laughed at her own joke and wandered off on the arm of a rather wrinkly looking Ned Stark. They both gave him a backward glance, still a little concerned, and Gill nodded weakly, feeling his cheeks flame bright red under all the theatrical paint and latex. He could see Eric, Dinah and the others looking at him, different expressions on their faces and he straightened up and walked over. The dream fantasy in his head popped in a puff of smoke.

'Gill!' Eric said, over the top. 'Don't come too close, 'cos I might have to run you through with my dragon glass sword!' He put his hand on the sword handle tucked to his side and thrust his hips towards Gill aggressively. The whole thing was a joke - the bloke might as well pee on Dinah to mark his territory. Gill wanted to smack him over the head with his fake rubber phallus orientated weapon, but he didn't. He actually said nothing, just laughed weakly. Dinah laughed too, but he couldn't tell whether she was doing it to be polite or she actually found it funny.

'So,' Gill said, eager to move past the thrusting, 'you all having a good day so far?'

Dinah smiled then, and it lit up her eyes. 'Yes, it's been fab so far, and someone said they thought they saw Kit Harington!'

Eric guffawed, punching Gill on the shoulder. 'I already told her Gilly, I'm here baby!'

Gill rubbed his shoulder where it smarted. 'Yes, ha ha, but actually it's Gill.'

'What?' Eric said, looking over Gill's shoulder. 'Hey Eddie! Come to join my watch, have you?' He punched Gill on the same shoulder, in the same spot, and turning to wink at Dinah, swaggered over to a couple of men dressed as members of Castle Black. He could still be heard posturing and preening from a few stands over.

'He gets quite into all this,' she said, rolling her eyes. She and Eric had been dating for nearly two years, two years of torture for Gill. He had met her online, chatting in an online Star Wars forum, and they had found that they had mutual friends in common, and lived near each other. He would never forget that first time he met her in person, in the coffee shop in town. He had been in love by the time the order was placed. She had started dating Eric two weeks before. Sometimes time and fate were just not your friend. He had been friend zoned by the time their coffees had cooled.

'Yeah,' Gill said. 'I noticed. You come together?'

'I got a lift with him; my car is in the shop again. I won't get it back for a few days, so it was nice that he was off work. Mum hasn't been too good.' She looked a little sad. Gill resisted the urge to close the gap between them and cuddle her.

'How is Elaine?' he asked kindly.

'Aww, you remembered her name!' Dinah looked pleased. 'She really liked you, you know, when you dropped me off that time.' Her smile faded. 'She's getting worse to be honest, I was thinking about getting a flat nearby, but I think it's just better if I stay around to be honest.'

Gill nodded. Elaine hadn't been the same since Elliott, Dinah's younger brother, had died in an accident while travelling five years ago. Dinah had moved in with her to see her through it, but years later, she was still there, and the house she had bought for herself and her future was sold on. Now she was kind of in limbo, but family came first, it had always been just the three of them. How could she leave her mother with no-one? He wanted to ask her why she was considering getting her own flat, and not moving in with Eric, but he didn't want to know the answer. Or set a seed growing in their heads.

'On the bright side, it does save me a pretty penny on expenses, so I can afford stuff like this!' She did a little excited hop and a twirl, giggling to herself. Gill said nothing, because he was in another montage. This time, Dinah was moving in slow motion, sparks flying from her in gold flecks, the song 'Dream Weaver' playing in his head. She opened her mouth slowly, and he smiled lazily at her lips.

'Gill, you there?' Dinah was suddenly stood still, looking at him with a puzzled look on her face. 'Where did you go then?'

Gill shrugged. 'Sorry, er…listen, shall we have a look

around?' He glanced furtively over his shoulder, but Eric was busy showing a blonde dressed as an alien his legs, clad in black tights. The man was a putz. What the hell did Dinah see in him?

He lead Dinah away. He lived for his weekends, for these events. And for seeing her. If only she would notice him. Why did the women he liked always like someone else? Someone that treated them like dirt, and didn't respect them?

'Er yeah, just a minute. Eric and I have plans later, so I don't want to wander off and be rude when we came together.' Gill nodded, flashing her a fake smile. Sure, run after him, like always.

Gill Cohen was the typical bachelor, albeit a reluctant Jewish bachelor, which meant that his mother and father, Ira and Abela, were in despair. His mother had even made the comment last week that if he didn't start using his man parts soon, he would lose them.

'Gill!' She said, raising her hands in frustrated circles in her kitchen. Her wooden spoon splashed passata all over the kitchen cupboards nearby, but she didn't notice. Gill stood there looking sheepish, watching her cat, Barry Manilow, licking it off the ceramic tiled floor.

'Gill,' she repeated for effect, slamming the spoon back into her oversized saucepan and looking at him over her glasses. 'If you don't find a girl to marry soon, you might as well take your little gonads and put them up on the shelf, eh? What good will they be without a woman, and with you wearing the skinny jeans and the tightie whities, you are choking my grandchildren!'

'Mum, come on! It's not that easy!'

'David did it!' She said, as if that was the answer to

everything. David was always the answer to everything, like a yardstick that his mother measured her son against. He was his mum's dearest friend's son, now happily and newly married to a Jewish girl.

'Mum, David fell in love. His mother trawled the whole of Yorkshire to find him a Jewish woman and he happened to find the one, it narrows the odds somewhat!'

'Ohhhh!' she said, her arms flicking the spoon with force again. A stray piece of chopped mushroom hit Barry on the back of his head, but he just glowered at Gill and continued to eat. 'So, it's mine and your father's fault, is it? You need to date, not spend your time with these silly sky-fi things!' Another hand flick. Gill wiped a drip of tomato juice from his shirt and tried not to roll his eyes at his mother.

'It's sci-fi Mum, and I love doing that, you know I do. And there are girls there.'

Abela snorted. 'Yeah, girls who spend their weekends dipped in paint and wearing tiny pieces of cloth. They might as well dance on a pole. At least they would make money then, eh Ira?' She laughed and looked through the kitchen doors to the conservatory, where her husband was sat going through some paperwork.

'Gill, did you see the MiniSave shop accounts this quarter? I swear, the man doesn't know how to use his own damn till, but he makes a killing!'

'Ira, never mind the damn accounts. What about our grandchildren?'

'Eh,' Ira said, looking around him as if a bouncing baby or two had just walked in. 'What grandchildren? Gill, get in here and look at these!'

'Ira!' Abela scolded. 'I want grandchildren, will you talk to our son? I am ready to knit, and bake, and look after my grandbabies, not look at your fat head till they cart me out in a box!'

'Oy woman, give the poor boy a break! He will find his own woman in his own time!'

'He's nearly 40!'

'32!' countered Gill, but he was ignored. His mother was stirring her pot now, her bosom jiggling hard from side to side as she worked on making a hole in the base.

'What am I supposed to do? Let him get on with it? I will have the reaper knocking on this door before the stork. Talk to your son!'

Ira threw his arms up in the air, the piece of paper fluttering to the floor. 'Fine! Fine! Gill, you have six months to find a wife, or face the consequences!'

Gill, accustomed to playing tennis neck, looking in bemusement from parent to parent as they bickered, swung his head to his father in surprise. 'Wait, what?'

Ira, oblivious as always, turned to Gill.

'What's this about a grandchild? You finally got a girl to notice you?'

Gill sighed. It was going to be a long dinner.

***

Monday

Gill walked into the office, slammed his laptop bag down on the table, and threw himself down in his chair. Rory looked over his glasses at him.

'Good morning, eh?'

'My morning was fine, besides the fact that my mother sent

me a text message at seven o'clock with a link to an article about declining sperm potency in the over 30s.'

'Nice, skipped the porridge, I bet?'

'Er yeah, after that, I had a banana and some toast. Gave eggs a swerve too.' Rory's lip twitched, and he looked back at his paperwork.

'Still on your case then?'

Gill walked over to the coffee machine and poured himself a cup. 'Coffee?'

Rory shook his head. 'Already had three. Better not.'

'Bad morning for you too?'

'Bad weekend. Eric and Dinah?'

Gill pulled a face. 'Huh-huh. Mum too.'

'Ah,' Rory acknowledged. 'Gotcha. Well I had the plumber from hell, my dad is having more sex than I am, and the girl I like doesn't know I exist. Other than that, all good here.'

Gill slumped back behind his desk and slurped his coffee. 'What the hell are we doing wrong, Ror?'

'You got me there. Sarah has a theory though.'

'Really?' Gill said, intrigued. 'The hot girl you have been friends with forever has a theory on why you're alone. Do tell.'

'Give over, I told you, Sarah's a friend. She was talking about Sasha. She thinks that we're too nice.'

'No shit,' Gill said. 'Eric is a douche, and he still has a girlfriend. What's her point?'

'That is her point. Women don't want the nice guys, they want the bad boys. Think about it…Eric - dickhead, right? Has Dinah. You're friend zoned. Greg – douchebag - but Sarah still dated AND had Annabel with him. My dad!' Rory jabbed the air with his finger, warming to his theme. 'My dad is a walking hard-on, and he gets all the women.'

Gill gave a hollow laugh. 'Right, so we just play douchebags, and get the girls. Right? Easy?'

Rory looked across. 'No, but we wise up. I'm in a rut, and so are you. Let's stop being so available, treat them mean to keep them keen. We don't have to be evil, or nasty, but let's play the game. What do you say?'

Gill said nothing, but a text sounded on his phone. Pulling it from his pocket, he read a text, dropping his head to his chest.

'My mother just sent me a link to a Jewish dating site for the over 30s. Apparently, they do a month's free trial.'

Rory grimaced at his friend. 'Ouch. You in then?'

Gill nodded, dropping his phone into his top drawer and slamming it shut. 'I am so in.'

Monday lunchtime, and Rory was stood clutching a tan handbag in Leeds city shopping centre.

'Sar, I only get an hour for lunch, you know that, right?'

Sarah ignored him as she swept around him like a typhoon, picking clothes from rails and draping them over her arm. 'Er, you're the boss. I'm pretty sure Gill can handle the phones for a bit longer. I swear, you two are workaholics. This is so hot, oooh, and this, and this,' she mumbled excitedly, pausing to pick a dark pink paisley shirt off the rack.

'No! Really?' Rory frowned. 'It's a bit girly isn't it?'

Sarah scrunched up her eyebrows, adding a pair of skinny

jeans to the pile that looked like they had lost a fight with a lawnmower. 'Ror, men wear playsuits these days, and have man buns. A few pairs of jeans and a nice shirt won't do you any harm.'

'Do me any harm?' he echoed in disbelief, pulling at his suddenly too tight white shirt collar. He was wearing his usual office outfit of shirt, tie, smart trousers and v neck blazer. He looked like a grandad a little, albeit a hot one. Sarah watched him over the racks as she moved around, taking in his trim stomach and thick hair. With his glasses, he did look like pre-transformation Clark Kent. As she watched him look in horror at a t-shirt bedecked in sparkly skulls and faux chain-mail, she realised how attractive he was, objectively speaking of course. Looking at him like an available woman that wasn't his best friend, of course. He deserved a good woman, but she didn't see him with Sasha. He was gentle, caring. She just seemed to crave attention. Sarah saw her in the club, schmoozing the clients, lapping up the compliments from her ever adoring crowd. The girl was paid to party, to make others look good. It didn't scream future Mrs Gallant. Being a good friend, she should just tell him. Really tell him, rather than the subtle hints she dropped at him.

'Sarah?' He called, pulling her away from her thoughts of kicking puppies. 'Please, for my sake, nothing with diamante, okay?'

An hour later, Rory was sat in Antoine's chair at the salon, looking a little shell shocked. Sarah was sitting in a chair next to him, drinking a latte with her feet up.

'Sarah,' he said nervously, looking around him at the dye charts and frenzied activity around him. 'What are we doing in this place? I should be at work you know.'

Antoine's was the best in Leeds bar none. Sarah went to

college with his daughter, and Antoine had taken a shine to her one day in the college car park, watching her juggle her busy life. Antoine had been a single father, raising his daughters Isabella and Francesca alone whilst running a busy cutting-edge salon. He knew a kindred spirit when he saw one. So now, he forced the odd free haircut on Sarah, and she actually reluctantly agreed from time to time.

'Rory, you own half the firm. You can take an afternoon off once in a while, and I'm not in college today. Class was cancelled. Mum is picking Annabel up for me. You wanted a plan, now you have to stick to it. Text Gill, let him know. He can do the same another day.'

Rory groaned, and opened up his mouth to say more, but Sarah was already laid back in her chair, eyes closed, coffee resting on her lap. She looked so pretty today, relaxed for once. Rory was so used to worrying about her, he didn't see how well she looked when she wasn't stressed. It was a look he wanted to see more of.

'Thanks for today,' he said, but the noise of the dryers and the chatter of people whipped the words round in the air. She didn't respond. He leant forward, taking the coffee cup from her. She was asleep. He smiled, taking off his blazer and wrapping it around her. The woman was so tired, she could sleep through anything.

'Hello!' A man in a ruffled white silk shirt said. Rory jumped up from his chair, shushing him.

'Shhh! Sorry, it's just she doesn't sleep much.'

Antoine nodded, smiling down at the sleeping woman. 'I know how she feels, bless her little cotton socks. So,' he said, waving his hands theatrically but keeping his voice low. 'Sarah tells me you need to find a woman and need a makeover.'

Rory grimaced. 'Er...well...one woman really, and to be fair, I don't think I need anything drastic.'

'Oh,' Antoine pouted, pulling Rory into the chair. He pinned him to the back rest with his slender fingers, and without ceremony ripped a tuft of hair out by the root.

'Mmmmffff!' He screamed through muffled lips, not wanting to wake Sarah. This man was no hairdresser, he was a butcher! Antoine raised a finger as if to silence. 'Please, silly man. It's a lock of hair! I have to see the damage for myself before we start the repair.'

Rory sank lower into his chair as he watched his poor follicles being scrutinised. His head throbbed, and he daren't touch his scalp, but he was pretty sure he now had a bald patch AND crap hair. AND a new wardrobe that would make Alice Cooper think twice about wearing it. He was pretty sure he saw Sarah shove the sparkly skull monstrosity into one of the bags. The plan was going well so far. Day one, and he already wanted to reach for the rip cord and curl up in his comfy cardigan.

'Oh, tut tut, Rory,' Antoine chided, shaking his head. He held the little tuft of hair aloft as though it was a dog turd between his fingers. 'This is reaaallly bad, you should have come much sooner. I don't know what to tell you.'

'Er, I think we can just go with a wash and a trim, something a bit more modern perhaps?'

Antoine was already shaking his head. He clicked his fingers and a rather glamorous assistant appeared from nowhere. 'Dispose of this,' he said, putting Rory's hair tuft into her outstretched palm as though it were a grenade, 'and bring me the emergency highlight chart.'

Rory could hear himself scream silently in his head, and he

gripped the hand rests for dear life. All this, and he still needed a play to get the girl. Something told him it would take more than a makeover to impress the lovely Sasha Birkenstock.

CHAPTER SEVEN

Monday - a week later

Greg Beckett really did lead a charmed life. He had his dream job, and women on tap. All he had to do was flash them a smile and tell them what he did for a living, and they were putty in his hands. The sun was shining, and he had the top down on his BMW, enjoying the admiring glances of the people in Leeds City Centre. One older woman even air punched him as he went past, shaking her fist at him rapidly as he skimmed through the puddles from the early morning rain with his wheels. People sure loved him. He waved at the woman, and she waved back, wildly trying to get his attention. He tooted as he turned the corner. 'Sorry baby, I'm on my way to pick up a cracker!'

He drove out of the ring road into the suburbs and whacked the radio up loud, singing along as he navigated his bright red car towards its destination. Pulling up in a side street, he turned off the engine and checked his reflection in the central mirror. He flashed his teeth, pulling a face like a laughing horse, and picked at a non-existent speck on his pearly teeth. Smoothing his brows with spread fingers, he finger gunned his reflection in the mirror and winked. He positively strode to the primary school, feeling like he was cock of the walk. Today he had agreed to pick up Annabel as Sarah was off doing her little college thingy, and he planned to take her for a drive and a cheeky pint and a bit of food at the local country pub franchise. Save him cooking, and Annabel liked to be seen out with her daddy anyway, plus it didn't hurt that the barmaid was a tasty piece. He figured the 'doting single father' angle might just clinch the deal. He was just walking through the playground when he stopped dead. Bunny was there, talking to the other mothers. She was laughing at something one of them had said, when she spied him, and her face dropped.

'Greg, why are you here? You were on pick up tomorrow, have you forgotten?'

Bless her. She's confused. Easy done when you're an interfering old bat. He smiled condescendingly as he neared the coven.

'She just had a holiday from school too. Could you not have seen her then? Phone broken, is it? Or are your thumbs singed?'

The women all narrowed their eyes and flanked Bunny, who was looking positively furious.

'No, I haven't forgotten,' he simpered, using air quotes to punctuate 'forgotten'. 'I had to work last week, fighting fires.' He winked at the ladies, but they looked at him like he had just flung his own poo at them. Like the ape they seemed to think he was. 'It's my day, Sarah texted me to pick up my girl. We're off out for tea.'

The women around Bunny all folded their arms at the same time, and the effect was unsettling, like swords being drawn or shields being raised.

'Oh,' Bunny said in a high-pitched voice. 'Pub again, is it? Annabel hates that place Greg, and you're never going to trick that girl into sleeping with you. She's Xander's aunt. Isn't that right, Jess?'

A woman stepped forward, lithe and blonde, dressed in full gym gear. 'Yes, that's right. She saw through you on the first day, Greg.'

Greg looked at the women, all glaring at him in contempt. He wasn't used to women looking at him like this. Usually it was sexy smiles and come to bed eyes, not daggers and angry body language. These women looked like they were wishing for a length of rope and four horses to appear.

'I'm wounded, ladies,' he punctuated this by clutching at his chest. 'I only go there because Annabel loves the food.'

'She really doesn't, Greg - you should actually listen to what your daughter says.'

Greg's eyes darkened. This was starting to annoy him now. He didn't like being called out on his parenting. He saw it as a badge of manhood, the fact he had a daughter. Women loved the single dad angle. They didn't need to know she didn't live with him.

'Bunny, it's my day for having Annabel. I'm here for her.' His voice was lowered, a slight growl to its edge. The women all took a step closer to Bunny, but she was already moving forward, finger jabbing at him.

'Don't you dare try to intimidate me, Greg. I have eaten bigger things than you for breakfast sonny Jim, Annabel is with me today. She has a birthday party to go to, and she's not missing that to help you pull women. Now leave, before she comes out.'

She jabbed a finger into his chest, her jaw set, and the bell punctuated the silence. Greg wanted to grab her finger, give them all a piece of his mind, but he turned around instead and stormed back to his car.

The women all watched him leave, Angie putting an arm around Bunny, who was shaking with adrenaline and anger.

'God Bunny, I knew he was a dick, but he looked violent then. He hasn't hit Sarah, has he?'

Bunny tried to shake off the feeling of dread she felt as she watched Greg driving off at speed in his dickhead mobile. She had a flashback to a night, a long time ago. Annabel was just a babe in arms, and they had gone to spend the weekend with Greg.

They had been talking about moving in together, into Greg's flat, but Sarah wanted to take things slowly. Wise move, given that Greg seemed to spend most of his time at his mother's. She was being sensible as always, wanting to make sure it was the right thing with Annabel being such a surprise, and an adjustment. Sarah wanted the next move to be the right one for all of them. This weekend together was a first tentative step, a toe dipped into the water.

Bunny was fast asleep, propped up in bed, book on her lap, glasses askew. She had taken a big glass of wine and the latest steamy romance novel to bed; the dull Saturday weather having kept her indoors pottering around her big house all day. It had been a bit of a weird day for her too. Eerily quiet. She was awoken by the sound of desperate hammering at the door and picking up the cricket bat she kept at the side of her bed, she headed down the stairs, listening. Then she heard it, a baby's anguished wail, her daughter's panicked voice.

'Mum, it's me!'

She gripped the bat and flew to the door, unlocking it as fast as she could. Throwing it wide, she pulled her soaking wet children into her home and stepped outside. She raised the bat, swinging it from side to side. There was no-one on the porch. She locked up and dropping the bat, ran to the kitchen, where Sarah was busy trying to undress a very wet and screaming Annabel. Bunny took one look at the pair, and instincts took over. Sarah never stayed at Greg's again, and Annabel only went for hours at a time. The relationship between them was seemingly over after that, and from then on, the tone in her voice changed whenever she spoke to him. She always seemed a little uncomfortable, and she never spoke of any plans. Bunny didn't ask what had gone on. She knew the answer wouldn't be good. All talk of her moving out was gone. That was answer enough for Bunny. Annabel's sweet little voice pulled Bunny out of her daymare.

'Nana, what's the matter? We need to go, the party's soon.' She felt a tug on her arm, and she bent down, ignoring the creak of her knees as she scooped up her beloved grandchild.

'Nanniiiee!' Annabel protested, as Bunny squeezed her tight. 'You're crushing my sternum!'

Bunny chuckled, releasing her a little and rubbing her nose against hers. Annabel giggled, loving their little Eskimo kisses. Nana was the one person who got the girly side of Annabel, as long as no-one was watching. Her face changed from laughter to a determined stance, and Bunny mirrored her, making her laugh again. She knitted her little eyebrows together, pouting her little lips, and Bunny's heart swelled.

'Nana, in all seriousness, we need to hurry. I'm telling you now though, I am NOT wearing a dress.'

Bunny was still laughing halfway home, and Annabel had a lovely time at her friend's party. In jeans, and a Doctor Who t-shirt.

***

Pulling up outside his house with a screech of tyres, Greg was just about to fire off an angry text to Sarah when he saw her last one to him.

Please Greg, don't forget. ANNABEL PICK UP - TUESDAY AFTERNOON - SCHOOL. Don't let her have coffee again.

Shit. Bunny was right. Fan-freaking-tastic. He would never hear the end of this now. Just what he needed. When the hell did these women start being lippy, thinking they knew best? Greg sent a text anyway, wanting to vent and get the last word in.

Sarah, tell your mother to stop interfering in my life. I can't have Annabel tomorrow now, called into work.

There. Let Sarah sort childcare out. He was no-one's fool. He grinned at his phone, and he strode to his pad to crack open a beer, clicking his car locked over his shoulder. One to the Gregster.

***

'So,' Rory said some time later. 'What do you think?'

Turning to Sarah, who was now awake and staring at her phone, he showed off his new shorter, spikier haircut.

'Mother fucker!' she shouted, punching the chair with her fist.

Antoine and Rory looked at each other bug eyed in the mirror.

'Er, I don't think it's that bad, I rather like it,' Rory assured Antoine who was looking decidedly put out. Sarah looked up from her phone and her expression softened.

'Sorry! Antoine, I am so sorry. It looks great, Rory. It's just Greg. He had a run in with Mum and now he won't have Annabel tomorrow. I have late lectures. Oh, I could kill him!'

Rory sighed. 'I can get Annabel from school tomorrow, don't worry. She can come to mine, okay?'

Sarah looked at him, still angry with Greg. It showed on her face, and Rory wished that Greg would just disappear. They were supposed to be making their amicable ex/co-parenting work for the sake of their daughter, but all Greg seemed to excel at was bedding women and making a swift exit from the women in his life. He walked over to her, and Antoine drifted away, letting them talk. Rory rounded the chair, taking Sarah into his arms without asking. She let out a frustrated sigh.

‘Ror, what the fuck am I doing? I don't want to be with Greg, but now I’m stuck with him for life. He literally screws anything with a pulse, and still wants me to give him another chance. I really think he just wants someone to wash his pants and put up with his shit. I'm trapped. Annabel deserves so much better, but my mum deserves a life of her own too. I'm burdening everyone, and I'm exhausted!’

She let out a sob, and Rory pulled her closer to his chest, shushing her and rubbing her shoulder. He motioned to Antoine and passed him his credit card with an apologetic smile. He took the card and waved away his apology, passing him a business card in return.

Rory pulled her towards the door, picking up her handbag and shopping bags as he tucked her into his side. They paid up and waving a quick goodbye, Rory grabbed her hand and they walked towards his car. He folded her into the passenger seat like she was a child and threw the bags into the boot. Taking his seat next to her, he clicked on his own seatbelt and pulled out of the car park. He put the radio on low, an easy listening local radio station he always listened to, but this time he did it to cover the sound of his best friend crying. He knew she hated looking weak, even with him. He said nothing to her, just headed straight for his house. Sarah looked up once, saw where he was going and looked at him with red eyes.

'Don't you have to work?' He looked at her and shook his head. She smiled at him weakly, and he covered her hands with his, bringing one with him when he shifted gears. They drove the whole way home like this. Every pedestrian's face turned into Greg's. It was a miracle Rory got them home safe. But that was Rory, Mr safe and dependable. Just like the lothario plumber had said. Rory would have laughed if he didn't find it quite so pathetic.

***

'Do you want me to ring Dad, tell him you can't work tonight?'

She shook her head, not that he expected her to say any different. She was ensconced on his couch, cup of tea and ham sandwich set out on the coffee table.

'I need the money. Plus, I'm looking forward to the debut of Rory mark II.'

He groaned in response. 'Are you sure about this? I don't want to look stupid. What will Dad say, anyway? I don't want to look like him.'

Sarah snorted her tea. 'Look like your Dad? Rory, don't be a div! You'll look hot, trust me!' She cleared her throat and shoved a corner of the sarnie into her mouth. Hot? Me look hot? Does she think that I do? Rory looked at her in question, but she was reaching for the remote.

He turned to the mirror in the hallway, looking at himself up and down. Wearing his usual work wear, he looked odd. Like someone had swopped his head for another, like a Ken doll. He looked once more at the bags by the front door. Maybe it was time to see just what he was going to be wearing.

'I'm going to go try some of these things on,' he called into the lounge.

'Okay, come down and show me though. I'm just going to phone Mum and Annabel.'

'Okay,' he replied, grabbing the bags. 'And listen, if you want, Annabel can stay here tomorrow, I'll take her to school. That way when you get back from college you and Bunny can have the night off.'

There was no reply. Rory shrugged and walked up the stairs. 'I'll take that as a yes. Don't argue.'

Rory didn't see Sarah wipe another tear away and thank her lucky stars that not all men were total shits. She called her mother, to discuss the sack of crap she HAD spawned her daughter with.

***

Sarah arrived home and waved to Rory as he pulled away. She had ended up falling asleep on the couch, waking up when Rory awoke her with a cup of coffee telling her it was time to get back to see Annabel before she went to work.

'I'm back!' she trilled, dumping her keys in the bowl on the hall table.

'Hi darling, you have a good day with Rory?' Her mum called from the kitchen.

'Yeah,' Sarah smiled, thinking of how Rory had looked after her. 'I did. Where's Annabel?'

Her mother came through to the hallway, tea towel in hand.

'She's upstairs watching David Attenborough with her headphones on. She had a great time at the party. The mothers are lovely at that school.'

Sarah nodded, and they both went through to the kitchen. 'She wasn't mortally wounded by her dad showing up then?'

'No love,' Bunny shrugged, pouring a pot of tea from the pot. 'She didn't see him, he was gone before she came out and I didn't tell her. I haven't told her he's not coming tomorrow either. Did you get sorted?'

Sarah nodded, sitting down on a dining room chair and holding the warm tea gratefully. 'Rory is going to pick her up and have her for the night, so I can sleep. I didn't ask, he offered. He's going to go and buy Princess Diaries. He googled it,' she giggled.

Bunny smiled. 'I swear, that man is wrapped around her little finger.'

Sarah nodded, sipping her tea. 'I know, she's doing better than her mother. The men in my life are shits.'

Bunny gave her a stern look. 'Man, love. Singular. Or should I say, man child. Are you really going to get back with him one day? I don't see what you're doing it for, you're either together or you're not. What's with all the fannying around?'

'Mum, do you want rid of us or something?' Sarah looked worried for a moment, and Bunny's heart squeezed. She wished her Charlie was here, he would have boxed Greg's wet ears and sent him packing the minute he upset his daughter. Bunny felt so mad sometimes, watching her daughter put her life on hold for a man who couldn't give a toss. They were accessories to him, like his penis extension of a car, and Bunny didn't like it one bit. She sat down at the table, turning down her stewpot, and put her hand over her daughter's.

'Love, you and Annabel have a home here forever, that's not in question. I love having you both, it keeps me company and I like helping you. I just don't want you putting your life on hold for anyone. You know what your dad said, before he went.'

Sarah's eyes teared up, and she blinked them away. 'Live a big life my girl, and if someone stands in your way -'

'Kick them in the balls!' Annabel said, walking into the kitchen and nestling into her mother's arms. Sarah and Bunny laughed, and Sarah dropped a tea warm kiss on her daughter's soft hair.

'That's right, my angel,' Bunny said, squeezing her daughter's hand.

'Why are you both sad? Is it because of Grandad?' Annabel asked the two teary women.

'We're not sad my girl, we're just making plans. Aren't we?' She looked at her daughter and saw her nodding.

'Yep,' said Sarah, lifting herself of the chair and putting Annabel in her place. 'I have to get ready for work now and get the ball rolling.'

Bunny grinned. 'Go get 'em!'

Annabel looked from woman to woman and frowned. She had heard the conversation about her dad. She didn't want her mum and dad to get back together. She loved her dad sure, but she had realised a long time ago that he wasn't the sharpest knife in the drawer, and not the nicest one either. She liked her life as it was, for the most part. Looking at her tired mum trudging up the stairs, and her grandmother humming and cooking away, she realised that she would have to make plans of her own. She knew just where to start too.

***

Walking into Miranda's that night, Rory felt like he was in costume. His legs felt like they were stuffed into drainpipes with his new skinny jeans, his shirt was so tight his nipples were protruding, and apparently socks were the devil and were not allowed to be worn with his new super trendy Oxfords. His eyes could feel every bit of wind and grit kicked up by the early evening traffic, though his jelled hair never moved, and he had reached up to push his glasses up his nose at least ten times in the past hour. His disposable contact lenses felt strange, and his spacial awareness was off. He had never realised how flat his glasses made everything. He had gone to step off the pavement and nearly fallen over. It felt like he had jumped into an abyss. Not to mention the fact that these were his fifth pair, having lost half of them on the bathroom floor.

He nodded to the girl on the door, walking like Bambi into the foyer, but he felt a heavy hand on his shoulder. Nathan the doorman was looking down on him, his head broadly perched on a wall of muscle.

'You have to pay to come in, pal.'

'Eh? Nathan?' Rory felt an odd satisfaction when he realised Nathan hadn't recognised him. At the sound of his voice, his expression changed from business like strength to confusion.

'Rory? That you?' Rory nodded.

'Yep, new outfit.'

Nathan looked him up and down, before slapping him on the back so hard he almost fell over.

'Dude, you look so different! You look awesome!'

Rory smiled, pleased that his efforts had been noticed, till he realised what it meant about his old look. Perhaps he had been fooling himself a little that his comfortable clothes were doing anything but blending him in with the background.

'Thanks,' he said and reciprocated the rather meaty fist bump. He turned and headed for the office, eager to get his paperwork done and make his entrance into the club once Sasha arrived. He could watch on the CCTV. Tonight was Operation Get Noticed. The truth was, Sasha did know who Rory was, they had spoken enough times. When she wanted to do a PR event at the club, it was often Rory she spoke to. Doug, to his credit, seemed to have realised that his son had a soft spot for her, and so he always seemed to magically make himself scarce when she wanted to have a meeting. Rory of course was only too happy to help, but she had yet to learn his real name, or in fact realise that he existed in the male and very dateable form. Tonight, he and Sarah planned to change that. She would notice him, if it killed him. Which, in these trousers, wouldn't be too hard to achieve.

Going through the corridors to the office, he nodded at several bar staff members as he walked past them, trying to ignore the odd looks they gave him. He had to act like he normally looked like this, for the plan. His dad would be the test, he knew that. Knocking loudly on the door, he went in slowly.

'Dad, I'm walking through the door. Door opening, me coming in.' He said this loudly, to make sure the occupants of the room would hear it. A female voice made him jump.

'Rory, stop being a tit and come in. Your dad's not in yet.' Sarah was sat on his desk, thumbing through a stack of delivery notes. She looked at him momentarily and looked quickly back at the paperwork. 'Your dad ordered a load of crappy arse flavour shots; do you know where he got them from? They need to go back, they're not worth whatever he paid for them.'

Rory went to sit down at his desk, and Sarah swivelled around to face him. He noticed with surprise that she was wearing a black skirt, legs on show, rather than her usual work slacks.

'A skirt?' He said dumbly. 'Why are you in a skirt?'

Sarah looked down at her own legs in mock surprise. 'OMG, you're right, how did I miss that?' She rolled her eyes, wrinkling her nose. Rory loved it when she did that, she did it when she was embarrassed and wanting to appear annoyed. She was such a tough cookie, on the outside at least, but he knew different. He had first seen it at school, when in year 5 chubby bully Wayne Ball had teased her for not having a dad. She had wrinkled her nose, walked right up to him and punched him square in the face, knocking him out cold. The school rejoiced. Even the head teacher Mr Billings looked a little impressed. Bunny had of course fought her corner, and she escaped with a minor rap on the knuckles. What everyone else didn't see was her frustrated, heartbroken tears later that night, on the way home from school. Rory had. They had walked home together, going to sit in their usual tree, and he had sat and held her till she cried it all out. They had never spoken about it, not even then, but now Rory was always the silent shoulder she needed. He liked being there for her. He just wished she would realise she had a new bully in her life, and he needed knocking out.

'Sorry,' he said, looking again at her legs. They were toned, smooth, not surprising really since the woman never sat down. 'You look nice, just - different.'

She narrowed her eyes at him. 'Different bad, or different good?'

'Different good, definitely. Sorry.' He noticed how long her legs were, how shapely they looked in her cute pumps.

'Rory, stop staring!' She flicked a balled up Post-It note at him. 'Do I need to get changed, is it that bad? I have my trousers and boots in my locker.' She jumped up off the desk and Rory put his hand out to stop her.

'No! I mean, no, don't do that. You look nice. I just didn't expect it.'

'You didn't expect me to look nice?' Another crumpled Post-It smacked him in the nose.

'No! I meant, oh you know what I meant.'

She giggled, and Rory relaxed.

'Git.' She said, looking him up and down for the first time. 'You can talk, you look like a Calvin Klein model!'

Rory brushed down his new white fitted shirt, which lay over tight black jeans and a pair of tan dress shoes.

'Do you think so? I feel a bit on show. I can't believe that you can't wear socks anymore either, I feel daft.'

'It's the fashion, darrrling,' she purred, flicking her hand out like a diva. 'You look hot.'

'Hot?' Rory raised a brow. Sarah concentrated her gaze on the invoices.

'Yeah, hot, nice, whatever. Can you help with these invoices?'

Rory came to stand next to her, taking half the pile and thumbing through. He caught a scent of her perfume and smiled. She still had the same light floral scent about her. It was a smell that he always thought of as being perfectly her. 'You smell nice. I think those shots are a freebie, one of Dad's rep friends.' He air quoted the 'friends' part and Sarah's face dawned in recognition.

'Thanks. Oh, so no cost? Well that's good then, because they are utter garbage. They taste like cheap kids sweets. We can sling them out cheap, get rid. We are not ordering anymore though, so don't let him, okay?' She turned to face him, and their noses almost touched. She looked at him in question.

'You smell different? What is it?'

Rory lifted his shirt a little to his nose and sniffed. 'It's that new stuff you told me about, I'm not sure it's quite me.'

'No, I like it. May I?' She went in closer, and her nose tip brushed his neck. Rory's mouth went dry, and he could feel himself shiver a little. Weird. She pulled back, and he found himself looking at her lips.

'It's nice,' she said, her voice sounding odd, deep. He was about to answer, to try and stop looking at his best friend's lips when the door opened.

'Oh, I'm sorry, am I interrupting?' Doug stood there, looking faintly amused and the two of them fell apart, Sarah banging her leg on the desk.

'Oww! Shit! Nooo, of course not-'

'Dad, don't be daft-' Rory slammed his poor un-socked toe on the table leg, and winced. They both spoke in unison, having sprang apart, showering the office with invoices.

'Bollocks!'

'Arse!'

They both fell to their knees and scrabbled for the papers,

promptly clunking their heads together and reciting another string of obscenities.

'Jolly good,' Doug said jovially. 'I'll just grab a scotch and come back.'

'Dad, you don't have to do that,' Rory said, the fluster evident in his shaky voice. He looked at the doorway, but Doug had gone. He looked at Sarah, trying to get a read on her expression, but she was back to business, putting the invoices in a neat pile on the desk.

'Sarah, I-'

'So!' She said loudly, brushing her hair back into place. 'Big plan tonight, eh? Phase 1? We need to get cracking, get the ball rolling.'

'Sarah-' Rory tried again, but she was already out the door.

'Don't forget, try to still be you, Ror. I better go set up the bar.'

She walked out of the office, and the door closed firmly behind her. Rory straightened up the rest of the papers and ran his hand through his hair. What the hell was that? He sat in his chair, taking a deep breath. It's Sarah, Rory. Sarah. He laughed to himself a little, at the absurdity of the moment, and a movement on the CCTV screen caught his eye. Sarah was outside the office door, talking to someone. He looked closer. She was alone in the corridor and pacing up and down. He realised she was talking to herself, occasionally putting her head in her hands. He looked at the door. Do I go talk to her? Apologise? Do I need to apologise? What even was that? He made a snap decision and went to stand, but when he opened the door, the corridor was empty.

CHAPTER EIGHT

Monday 8pm

'Darling, don't you worry yourself about these little details, that's what I'm here for.' Sasha trilled into her rose gold phone, the latest model of course, and smiled. 'No problem at all, love to Max.' She ended the call and sank back into the leather of her BMW, the latest model of course, in a gleaming two tone red colour. Another loaner from the car company client she had.

'Needy arsehole,' she muttered to herself. She had parked up outside Miranda's, ready for another night of smiling on command, getting people and brands noticed, promoting the things that the companies wanted the people to buy. She did it all, the cars, the gadgets, the jewellery. Everything she wore down to her designer underwear and the hair products on her luscious red locks were freebies, designed to get people reaching for their wallets and credit cards.

Tonight was no different, but it was a person that she was promoting this time. An up and coming boxer from Leeds, destined to be the next big thing, was doing a personal appearance, sponsored by Sasha's client, a well-known vodka company. So well-known that all the stars in LA were drinking it, Instagramming it, tweeting about it, and hash tagging it to death. All down to Sasha and her PR firm. Not bad for something made from potatoes. Now they were branching out into promoting people, and Sasha had agreed to take it on. The reality TV shows were big business in today's markets, and she wanted a slice of the action. If she could get people as clients, she could also get them promoting the brands. An up selling dream. She just had to get through tonight. The truth was, she just wanted to be in her PJs, at home with her pug, Radley. She was getting tired of being switched on 24/7. She never went anywhere mundane. Everything had to be amazing. After all, who wanted to see her buying Pot Noodles in Tesco? It had to be eggs Florentine and java at Gordon Ramsey's. St Tropez, not Blackpool beach. It was exhausting, and she wanted out. She wanted to be behind the scenes, let the people sell the brands. Truth was, she didn't want to work at all. The people she worked for sure had their worthy causes. Trophy wives, younger husbands, offspring cashing in on the name of their parent. Her father's infamy wasn't something she traded on apart from the odd menacing comment, but to be married to someone with money, status, bling? That would be the dream. For them, as well as her. She knew how to rock an outfit, shake a boudoir and run an A list event. What man wouldn't see that as a worthy trade?

At 17, she had been doing hair and beauty at college, dreaming of being the people in OK magazine. She wanted the finer things in life, but she didn't really want to work for them. Why do that, when she could get them for free? Early onset boobs had taught her a valuable lesson. There were two types of people in life - those who worked to get what they wanted, and the truly rich people. Rich with material goods, free time, travel opportunities. She saw it all the time in the media, on her television and in her mags - people jetting all over the world, blinged up. Did they work for it? Sure, but forty hours a week behind a desk working for other people just wasn't worth the payoff to Sasha. She wanted the big life, and she made it her mission to get it. The champagne lifestyle on a lager budget, or even better, for free.

Looking at herself in the mirror, she checked her reflection, slicked on another layer of lip plumping lipstick, and opening her door, she swung her heeled pins out and headed to the main doors. Tonight had to go well. She was looking for something exceptional to happen, and she had a feeling that tonight would be it.

Clicking her car key fob, she put them into her designer clutch and walked into the club. Miranda's was a hot spot; people seemed to gravitate towards this area of Leeds, and Miranda's was the jewel in the crown. It had a great VIP area, and this was just where she liked to do business. On show, but not with the usual crowds. Those behind the rope barrier were the ones to envy. She outsold two to one in this club. If she ever won the lottery, she would buy the place for herself, get someone in to run it. The potential was amazing.

Walking into the foyer, she nodded to Winston on the door, and he stamped her hand. She didn't pay here, another bonus. The owner had given her a free pass to come and go, as long as her clients didn't get rowdy. Tonight, she had booked the VIP area out for the boxer for the whole night, a nice weekday boost for the club. It worked better being quieter for events like this, and she had generated enough buzz to get things started.

'Instapic, Winston?'

Winston nodded, his dreads shaking. He pulled back his lips from his usual hard man expression to show two rows of pearly whites. Sasha sidled up to him, her coat slightly open to show the right amount of cleavage, tasteful, barely there. Enough to satisfy the zoomers.

'So, Leon in tonight, is he? I remember coaching him down the gym, doing well isn't he?' Winston boomed. He always boomed, even though he was speaking relatively quietly into her ear. She pouted, turning to her good side, snapping the picture and posting it over her social media, tagging Winston and Miranda's. She was a good people person, making it her business to befriend everyone. Twitter hated her, she was sure of it. She had almost spent as much time in twitter prison than her dad had in real prison. She pushed the vision of her father out of her head. She pecked Winston on the cheek, leaving a lippy mark.

'He certainly is, will you come and get a picture with him later? I'm sure he'd love to see one of his trainers.'

Winston beamed. 'Sure doll, that'll be nice. Cheers.'

Sasha smiled. 'Remember, if you ever want any new clients, I could do a profile for you.'

Winston nodded. 'Maybe, I'm pretty happy here to be honest.'

Sasha nodded. Winston was one of those talented people who never traded on it, just worked behind the scenes. She envied people like that sometimes, but the pull of the 'stuff' was just too great. She knew only too well what it was like to live without it, when her dad went inside. Never again.

She turned and headed inside, the early evening music pumping through the speakers. There were already a good few in, and she could tell by the way they were situated around the cordons that they were hoping for a glimpse of Leon. Leon Mendez was a sight to behold, apparently, not that Sasha had set eyes on him in the flesh. She normally did a meet and greet meeting with clients, but with him being so busy, and this wing of her business being a fledgling aspect, she was going in somewhat blind. It made her uneasy, but from his promotional materials, she knew he was easy on the eye. Silky voiced over the phone. Flirty, with good banter. An easy sell in her job.

She walked to the cloakroom, handing the usual usher her faux fur coat and clutch, making sure to pull out her phone to take with her. She tucked it into a zipped pocket in her dress. Custom made of course. The dress was so tight it was a miracle that she could even get a coin in there, let alone a large smartphone, but her alterations lady was amazing. She headed to the bar, and saw Sarah slinging drinks.

'Hey Sarah!' she said, in the voice she saved for her best gal pals.

Sarah glanced at her, smiling. 'Hey Sasha, you all ready for tonight?'

Sasha nodded. 'Yep, he's due to arrive on time, there should be a big crowd.'

'Aww good, listen, there is another VIP in tonight too, he's taken the smaller VIP area next to yours, but he shouldn't be there too long. Quick in and out thing, bit hush hush.'

Sasha looked at the VIP area but couldn't see anything over the crowd of people there. A mixture of men and women, all dressed in fancy dresses and smart suits. Odd looking, but something kept her watching. A man seemed to sit in the centre of it all, and she had the odd feeling that she had seen him before. Looking back at Sarah, she tried to hide her frown. Not good for her Botox for a start.

'What was the event for again?'

Sarah nodded to a waiter, passing him a tray of shots. 'It's need to know I'm afraid, but they're ordering these new shots like nobody's business. I hope we have enough for your event.'

Sasha's eyes bulged. 'Need to know? I need to know! What new shots? Can we get more?'

Sarah shook her head. 'To be honest, they're new on the market, bit of a retro taste. Like old style kids sweets, they're going mad for them. We got some in as a pre-emptive strike, before the buzz kicks off, but this guy seems to know what's in.'

'The guy in the white shirt?' She checked, turning back to the crowd and scrutinising his features again. She knew she had seen him before, but where? Something told her she needed to remember, and fast. Turning back to Sarah, she slammed her hands onto the bar.

'I'll buy the rest of the shots, whatever's left. Put it on my tab, okay?'

Sarah nodded. 'Sure thing, will do.' She motioned to Dean, who was setting more up on a tray. 'The rest of the retro shots are only for Sasha's party now, okay?'

Dean raised his eyebrows but nodded. 'No problem.' He finished filling the tray and called a waiter to take it to her area. Sasha sighed with relief. Crisis averted. What she didn't see as she took a selfie with the hashtag #retroshot, was Sarah's grin, and her nod to Rory, the man rocking the tight white shirt.

'It is working? Are we on?' Gill asked, looking decidedly uncomfortable under the flashing neon lights.

'Yep, looks like Sarah did it. You having fun?'

Gill looked at him as if he had asked if he wanted a nipple piercing. 'I'm coping, let's just say that. I see Eric is in his element.'

The men looked across from the booth to the front area, where Eric was holding court with the other cos-players. From the very animated story he was telling, it looked like he was trying to jump start a petrol mower whilst fighting off a shark.

'The man's a complete douchebag,' Rory said, rolling his eyes and knocking back one of the shots, knowing that Sasha had eyes on him. 'Now smile and take your medicine.'

Gill frowned at the glass. 'If this is the medicine, I would rather die from whatever's ailing me.' He knocked it back, giving his best impression of a man having fun. Rory laughed, patting him on the arm.

'Well done Gill. Why did you invite Eric anyway? I thought you hated him?'

'I do hate him. He's a complete div. I wanted Dinah to come, and where she goes, he follows.'

'Where's Dinah then?' Rory asked, nodding to the waiter who came to the table with a bottle of what he knew to be the most expensive bottle of champagne they stocked. He looked across at Sarah, but she just nodded to him professionally. He looked across the bar and saw Sasha stood there, raising a glass of bubbly to him. He gave her what he hoped was a nonchalant nod before quickly flicking his eyes away.

'I think she just sent this bottle over, what do I do?'

Gill tore his gaze away from the entrance doors and looked at him blankly. 'Sarah said to play the whole thing aloof, but I don't know. Maybe just send the waiter over to thank her. Or invite her over to drink it with us?'

Rory thought for a moment, watching Eric do his best impression of a man stuck in a box. What a tit. 'No, I'll just send the waiter to thank her, with no invitation or question as to who sent it, then keep ignoring her. As if we're not bothered, it works with the plan. We need her to feel like we aren't moved by her gesture, we get treated like that all the time. No biggie.'

Gill looked at him open mouthed. 'You're getting to be a bit Yoda at this stuff aren't you!?'

Rory's mouth twitched. 'I spent half the night researching first date etiquette online, so I now have a list of pretty much everything opposite. Sarah brought me an urban dictionary round too, do you know we are classed as hobosexuals?'

Gill drained his glass of champers in one. 'I have never, not even in accounting school!'

'HOBOsexual Gill, as in a person who doesn't really care about their appearance. The opposite of metrosexual.'

Gill looked utterly bemused. 'That's not a real thing.'

'It is,' Rory laughed. 'Honestly, you need to read that book. I felt like I had been doing my life all wrong.'

Gill shook his head and took another shot. 'I can speak Klingon, but the thought of learning all this lingo makes me feel odd.'

Rory laughed again, taking a shot for himself. Looking across, he saw that the boxer client of Sasha's had just arrived, and she was leading him to the VIP area nearby.

Gill was looking glumly at the door. 'Well, my night sucks. I'm a bit pissed, Dinah's not here and now apparently I'm a hopeless hobosexual.'

Eric appeared at his side, grinning. 'Mate, I'm so glad that you decided to come out and tell someone! I bet that's been killing you!' He guffawed with laughter and headed to the bar. Gill slammed his head on the table.

'Kill me now Rory. Just do it. A calculator in the back of the head a few times should do it.'

Rory pulled Gill's head up by his curly hair. 'Come on man, get it together.' He picked a piece of glitter in the shape of boxing gloves off Gill's sticky shot soaked forehead. 'Dinah said she would be here, so she will. I need your help, remember?'

Gill nodded dumbly. 'Sssrre thing, Rorrrr.'

Rory groaned. He was definitely worse for wear, and Gill was no drinker at the best of times. When they had been out for their work Christmas party (comprising of the two of them and Deirdre, the office cleaner) Gill had ended up doing his best Barbara Streisand on karaoke. Deirdre got a huge bonus that year. The two events were unrelated, of course.

'Giiill!' He stage whispered into his ear, not wanting to draw attention. To their credit, the other cosplay attendees were rocking the place, albeit with a few dodgy robot dance moves. He tucked the now sleeping Gill artfully into his seat, so he just looked like he was relaxing with the others.

It was time to make his exit. He nodded at Sarah, and she winked back.

***

Tuesday

Annabel sat in class, scribbling away in her notebook. Mrs Sims looked across at her, frowning. The rest of the class were quietly working on their worksheets while the timer ticked away.

'Annabel, you're supposed to be working, the timer is still on.'

Annabel lifted her head from her book and smiled. 'I've finished it, Miss.'

Mrs Sims smiled kindly. 'There are two sides to the sheet, dear.' Poor kids, they needed all the instructions. Being a supply teacher was a bit like babysitting the monkeys at the zoo sometimes. The girl looked wide eyed at her for a moment.

'I know that, I did both.'

Mrs Sims pursed her lips. 'Bring it to me then.'

Annabel stepped out from behind her desk, carefully closing her notebook and bringing the worksheet to her. She handed it to her and went and sat back down, continuing to scribble away. Mrs Sims frowned, looking at the worksheet, red pen in hand. Teachers weren't supposed to use red pen nowadays, because it was demoralising for children. Well, in her day, a little red pen went a long way to telling children just what was wrong with their work. All this precious snowflake business really got her goat. Pen poised, she looked at the sheet, her finger running down through the questions. Getting to the end of the sheet, she looked up at Annabel. She was still scribbling away. Clearing her throat, she turned the sheet around. Looking intently at the other side, she pursed her lips. Marking the sheet as 100% correct, she placed it in the in tray on her desk for the regular teacher to look at on her return.

Annabel looked around her, and then at the teacher. No-one else had finished yet, so she raised her hand.

'Yes,' Mrs Sims asked curtly. 'What is it?'

'Can I please go to the library? I need a book.'

Mrs Sims scowled. 'You are in the middle of a test!'

Annabel flinched at the tone in her voice. 'I finished my test, you have it there. I could stay in the library till the end.'

Mrs Sims shook her head vehemently. 'Rules are rules, Annabel, and just what are you writing in that notebook of yours?'

Annabel closed her book, crossing her arms over it. 'It's privatc Miss, but it has nothing to do with the test.'

'Oh, private is it?' She countered, doing her best impression of Miss Trunchbull. Or so it seemed to Annabel. She looked at the clock. It was 3pm. Rory would be here soon to take her to his house. She was counting down the minutes. As though punctuating her thoughts, the timer for the test went off on the teacher's desk. Mrs Sims banged her hand down on the alarm, making the children jump.

'Right,' she said, her voice now sickly sweet. 'Now children, come up and give me your papers, then get ready for home time. Pencils away in the pots please!'

Annabel sighed with relief, grabbing her notebook and getting ready to head to the cloakroom with the others.

'Not you,' Mrs Sims, jabbing her finger in Annabel's direction. Annabel looked at her classmates for help, but they were all already running for the cloakroom, heads down and Pokemon cards squirreled away. 'You my girl, can sit there and come to the doors with me. I want to speak with your parents.'

Annabel opened her mouth to speak, but Mrs Sims jabbed her finger up again to stop her. 'I'll take the notebook too.'

Annabel shook her head, gripping her book tighter. 'It's my book, not school's, and it's private.'

Mrs Sims' eyes bulged. 'Is that so?'

***

Rory pulled up to the school gates, a little early as usual. The truth was, the thought of him getting stuck in traffic and not being there with the parents when the gates opened worried him, so he always made sure to set off in plenty of time. He had already been shopping that day and was really looking forward to having Annabel for the whole night. He often volunteered, but Sarah was stubbornly independent, to the cost of her own health sometimes. Pulling a sleepover off would be some good brownie points for him with Annabel.

Walking up to the gates, he smiled at the mums and dads he recognised.

'Hey Rory,' Lee, one of the dads said, standing next to him. 'How's tricks? I almost didn't recognise you.'

'Oh thanks. I'm good thanks.'

'Been hitting the gym?'

'Er no…I don't do gyms to be honest.'

'You should come and train with me and Tim,' he nodded to one of the other dads, who was currently blowing raspberries on the tummy of a very giggly baby. 'He got me into it, the man's ripped. He's a personal trainer.'

Rory opened his mouth to say no, visions of him sweating and straining in a room full of Magic Mike extras, but another sound popped out.

'Yes, that'd be great.' He fished a business card out of his wallet. 'Give me a ring when you next go, and I'll sign up.'

Lee nodded. 'Cool. Hey, an accountant? You don't look like an accountant.'

Aside from the fact that not many people looked like their

jobs, apart from actor lookalikes, the Queen and the odd serial killer, Rory was absurdly pleased.

The doors opened, and the children started to come out, lunchboxes being slung at mothers, bags and coats being thrust into adult hands. The level of chatter was normally epic, but today Annabel's class seemed a little subdued. Rory noticed that they were coming out in single file like soldiers. Lee looked at him, and they exchanged a curious look. His son Adam came walking up and hugged his dad hard.

'Hey champ, you had a good day?'Adam looked to the door and curled a finger to his dad, beckoning him closer. Lee and Rory found themselves stooping to hear what he said.

'Mrs Sims is really mean. She won't let Annabel come out.' He poked Rory in his leg. 'You have to go save her.'

Lee hugged his son to him, picking him up into his arms. 'Substitute teacher mate, thinks she's the dog's gonads. Come on little fella, I think a trip to the sweetie shop on the way home might just cheer you up.' Rory nodded to him, and looking back to the doors, saw Annabel there looking wide eyed, clutching her things to her chest. She was stood next to a dragon. Fire breathing, ugly, scaly. This woman was a sight, and she was scanning the crowd like an assassin looking for her next target. Which, he realised as he got closer, was probably him. He suddenly wished he had bought a Kevlar vest along with his new wardrobe. He tucked his car keys into his hand and bounded up.

'Mrs Sims, is it?' I'm here to collect Annabel. Rory -' He held out his hand, but Mrs Sims cut him off, moving Annabel in front of her by her shoulders.

'Ah yes, well I have to say, Annabel hasn't had a good day today. Not at all, in fact.'Annabel looked like she was trying hard not to cry, and Rory reached out his hand for her. 'We need to discuss her behaviour, inside, if you will.' She seemed to pull Annabel back a step, away from him, and Rory frowned at her.

'What exactly is the problem? Annabel honey, come and stand with me.' He gently touched her arms and tucked her into his step, removing Mrs Sims' grasp.

'Well if you want to do this here, then fine. I'm afraid that Annabel has been very disruptive during a test, and quite insolent too. It seems your daughter has a problem with authority.'

'She's not -'

'I'm sure you are ready to defend your daughter, but really there is no defence.' The woman was thrusting her fingers out wide now, jabbing the air and Rory felt Annabel move closer to his side. He swallowed his annoyance and ignoring the teacher, he put his back to her and knelt down beside Annabel. She looked heartbroken, and Rory's heart squeezed. He hugged her to him, talking low.

'Belle, what happened honey?'

Annabel was shaking in his arms. 'I finished my test, so I started working in my notebook. I asked to go to the library, but she told me I wasn't allowed. She marked my test and then asked me for my notebook, but it's personal. Mum says that we're allowed to keep what we write to ourselves, so I said no. She got mad.' Her little voice choked, and Rory felt his anger rise. He stood up, taking her into his arms and eyed the teacher.

'You're new here, right?' Since you think I'm her father. Nice insult, by the way. I am much better than Greg the Smeghead. 'Supply teacher?'

Mrs Sims raised her chin slightly. 'Yes, that's correct.'

'Right,' Rory said, stroking the now quiet Annabel's hair. 'Well, don't expect to be coming into work tomorrow. You've made a little girl cry for wanting to get a book. Did she pass the test? I bet she got it all right, didn't she?'

Mrs Sims didn't answer, just set her jaw tight and swallowed.

'Well?' Rory pushed, fighting to control his own anger. Annabel had turned around now, watching the exchange for herself. He winked at her, wiping the tears from her eyes. She smiled at him, and his heart turned to gooey mush in his chest cavity. 'She passed 100% didn't she.' He said this as a statement, not a question and Mrs Sims nodded reluctantly.

'This little girl, who is my goddaughter, if you even bothered to check - nice safeguarding by the way - is bright, kind, and funny. For you - ' he jabbed his finger at her, 'to come in here and reduce her to tears like this for kicks is not on. I shall be speaking to her mother, and the Head. Not to mention the chair of governors, who is a personal friend of my father's. Now, I am late to take this little lady out for tea, and I am on the approved pick-up list, so at least you can't add child endangerment to your list of incompetence.' Annabel giggled, pushing her hand up to her mouth quickly to stop it. He whirled around, picking up Annabel's backpack and coat and throwing them both over his shoulder. Mrs Sims stood there spluttering, red faced. Rory hugged Annabel tight to him, searching her face for signs of distress. Annabel threw her arms around his neck, kissing him on the cheek.

'Thank you Uncle Roar-Roar, I had a horrible day.' Rory kissed her right back, blowing a raspberry and making her laugh out loud.

'Well Belle, you know what? Bad days make the good days all the sweeter, so don't you worry. I'll sort it.'

She smiled but then her face dropped. 'Dad will be mad.'

'Mad? For acing a test and being picked on by a mean teacher? I don't think so, Brain.'

She didn't reply, not looking convinced and Rory had to fight the urge to tell someone off again. It seemed that he always felt like that these days. He didn't know where this anger came from all of a sudden. He thought of his mother, always so calm and centred. Something he was, until recently. Perhaps it was going against her wishes that didn't sit with him right. Perhaps it was the layer of hair products on his scalp, all the chemicals doing things to his brain, firing his cylinders up all wrong. He wondered what his mother would think of what he was doing, the man he was. Would she be proud of the fledging new him, or be sad and mourn the loss of the man he was? Either way, she was gone now. She was gone, and he was alone, for the most part. Something that all his niceness had never been able to rectify. Maybe it wasn't what he planned for himself, but he didn't plan to rattle around in a big house all by himself at this stage either.

'Belle,' he said, stopping and turning her in his arms to face him. 'You did nothing wrong. Sometimes adults get things wrong, okay? Sometimes even we don't have all the answers. You weren't in the wrong here. Now, did Mummy tell you we had a sleepover planned for tonight?'

Belle's face lit up, her frown erased by her youthful toothy grin. 'I forgot! Can we watch National Geographic?'

Rory rolled his eyes. 'Come on, what do you think I am, a

rookie? I already downloaded the episodes. We can make fajitas, homemade guac, the whole enchilada. After bathtime I got Princess Diaries too, so I won't tell we watched if you don't.'

Belle bit the inside of her cheek. 'With popcorn?'

'Popcorn and face masks.' He held up his little finger. 'Pinkie vault?'

'Pinkie vault.'

***

Tuesday, and boredom meant wishing for a fire, a cat in a tree, a toddler's head stuck in a potty. Greg was annoyed. When Greg was annoyed, everyone knew about it. It was his way. What I feel, you feel. He didn't see an issue with that either. Surely the people in his life would always want to know just what was going on in his head? It was how he operated, and he didn't see a reason to stop. Except that lately, things were irritating him, more than the usual. Sarah for one. Work, for another. Do this paperwork, clean this, train up in that. To be a fireman was what he wanted. To be the guy who saved the families, got the cats out of the trees, made the girls swoon as he came down the pole. The reality was the boredom of it all. It wasn't like it was on the television. A lot of it was safety checks, building inspections, toeing the line with the chief. He was bored, truth be told. He always figured that one day, he would move on, do something else, but now it felt like time to move on, he had no clue what he wanted to do. Everything he wanted to do needed money, and he didn't have any.

Sarah was another flash point. She hadn't been answering his calls all day, and he knew that someone had to pick Annabel up, since he had cancelled on her. He knew it was Sarah's full college day though, so would she be with Bunny again? He had tried the house, but the old bag was obviously out or screening his calls, because he didn't get an answer. Leaving a message wasn't an option. One thing Greg wasn't was desperate.

CHAPTER NINE

Tuesday 9.30pm

Gill Cohen was desperate. His head still felt like cotton wool, his mouth was gritty. He had never really been hungover before, not in this league. This felt like his body was recovering from slow poisoning. Which in a way, it was. He was pretty sure he had developed an ulcer from burning off his stomach lining, and now his mother was trying to set him up with yet another debutante daughter from the synagogue.

'Ma,' he said pleadingly. 'I've had a very long day at work, and I'm pretty sure I'm coming down with something. Maybe death. Can we do this another time, please?'

'But Gill, this girl is perfect for you! I'm not even joking this time.'

'Oh really?' He said, walking from his kitchen with a hot cup of coffee and plonking himself down on his dark leather sofa. 'You said that last time, with the date from the bakery. She came covered in powdered sugar and talked about bread making all night.' His house was tidy as always, the TV paused on the latest action film on Netflix, and he had a takeaway on the way. He just wanted a night in to mourn the death of his liver and lick his wounds. His part of the plan had been a failure, and he needed to regroup. Tomorrow, he and Rory were going to put his part of the plan into effect, a plan to be aloof, suave and attractively unattainable with Dinah, a plan Gill had nicknamed the Cohen Caper. Gill smiled to himself at his choice of words. He felt like a superhero, or a spy. Hopefully at the end of it he would be a husband, and then his mother could obsess about him having kids instead. Same nagging, but with sex, to take the edge off.

'So? You don't want a career girl? You have a career.'

'Ma, I have no problem with women having careers. Of course, she should have a career, that wasn't the issue. The problem is I don't really care that much about bread, and I couldn't imagine talking about dough for the next fifty years.'

'Fine, fine.' He could see his mother now, zipping around the house in her heels. He could hear her bracelets jangling, so he knew she was probably dusting, or cooking. She was always doing something. The woman never stopped. When she woke up on a morning, she already had a list prepared in her head of the things she was going to do that day. Top of the list was normally 'find Gill a wife'. 'So, what about this girl then? She actually goes to - '

Gill's head pulsed. 'Ma, no! Please.'

'Arrgh, I swear Gill - please sort your life out. You can't marry your laptop you know.'

Gill threw back his head. 'I know Ma, and I do have a plan, okay? Give me some time. I like someone.' The line went quiet for a long time. 'Ma?'

'I think I died for a minute. Sorry. Did you say there was a girl?'

'A woman Ma, and yes.'

'An accountant?' She asked, warily.

'No Ma, not everyone works in accounting you know.'

'Not everyone is smart enough to work in accounting, this is true. Is she Jewish?'

Gill thought for a moment. Was she Jewish? Truth was, for the first time ever, when he met Dinah he hadn't actually given a second thought to that little detail. Truth was, if she was bright purple and ate rats he wouldn't care. He would like her no matter what. She did have a bit of baggage he wasn't so keen on though. A certain parasite called Eric.

'Gill, you there? Is she Jewish? Ira, get over here. Gill met a girl!'

'Yippee,' she heard him say from somewhere in their house. 'Free bagels for everyone!'

Gill heard a slap. 'Oy!' The line crinkled and banged as his two parents grappled with each other. He clicked the off button on his phone, and reaching over to the side table, clicked on the answering machine. Minutes later, he lifted his head off the couch cushion and opened his WhatsApp message. His mother.

WE WILL TALK LATER. CALL YOUR MOTHER X

He groaned, tapping out an 'OK MA'. He really needed to get her out of his hair. Now it was even worse, because he had to explain about Dinah having an Eric. As if summoned by his dilemma, Dinah's face flashed up on his phone, making him jump.

'Hello?' He said, squeaking. 'Hurr, hurr, hello?' He stood up quickly, combing his hair down with his free hand in the mirror on the wall, smoothing his shirt down. Dude, she can't see you on the phone. His reflection pulled the L sign on him.

'Gill, you there?' Dinah sounded off, odd. 'It's Dinah.'

Play it cool Gill. 'Dinah? Er...oh yeah. Hi, what's shaking?' Smooth Gill, smooth.

'I'm sorry to bother you but, I...I need some help. It's bad.'

Gill already had his car keys in his hand. The Cohen Caper was already gone out of his head. She needed him, he knew it, and he wanted to be there. He had never heard her sound so upset. It churned him up. 'You at home?'

'Yes,' she said, dissolving into tears. His spine had turned to ice water at the sound of her voice. He could tell that something was very wrong. 'Please, help me!'

'Dinah, I'm on my way. Stay on the phone, okay? Tell me what's wrong. My car kit will kick in, don't hang up, okay? Dinah?' Gill was frantic now, racing down the steps to his car. He pulled out onto the road, wishing he could be there, right now. Dinah was sobbing, and the sound panicked him. He hated it.

'Dinah, keep talking to me. Everything's okay, just tell me what happened.'

'It's Mum...s-she,' Dinah howled, and a tear rolled down Gill's cheek. He wiped it away, frustrated, trying to focus on the lamppost lit streets on the way to Dinah's.

'Who's with you, D? Is Eric there?'

'No, no it's just me and Mum-m-m. She's sick.' She hiccupped between bouts of crying. 'I didn't call him.'

She called me? Why, over Eric? Not the time Gill, not the time. Gill squashed down the burst of selfish pride he felt and pushed down on the accelerator. 'Okay, have you called an ambulance?'

Dinah was quiet for a moment, and Gill strained to hear her through the speakers over the noise of the car.

'Yes, but I think it's too late.' Gill pushed down harder on the accelerator.

Gill burst through the front door and headed straight up the stairs. The responder standing at the foot of the stairs yelped in surprise, but Gill ignored him, racing up the steps two and three at a time.

'I'm here, Dinah,' he called.

'Gill?' A tiny voice made him whirl around and there she was. She looked diminished, less somehow, like the life force had been dimmed inside her. He went to look into the bedroom, and a paramedic looked at him in question.

'Can I help?' he asked warily, making a motion to block Gill's path.

'I'm, I'm…' he said.

'He's with me,' Dinah said, her voice small. The paramedic looked at him, eyes scrunched up, and nodded, looking past him as another paramedic ran up the stairs with a blanket. Seconds later, the two men were carrying Dinah's mum down the stairs. Gill looked at Dinah, but she didn't look up.

The paramedic turned back to Gill as they raced out of the house. 'Meet you at the hospital?' he said in question, and Gill nodded back. 'We'll follow in the car.'

Gill's heart thudded into his shoes. The looks the paramedics gave each other didn't give him much hope. He turned around, taking a seat next to Dinah on the landing. She was still staring at her mother's bedroom door.

'Dinah,' he said softly, putting his hand over her clasped ones. 'We need to go hun, your mum's on her way. We need to get there.' No movement. She just stared ahead, and Gill wondered just how bad it was. Dinah loved her mother; for her to be like this, it must have been traumatic.

'Dinah,' he said again, firmer this time. 'We need to go.' He stood and pulled her arms up with him. She came without a fight, and Gill tucked his arm under hers, guiding her down the stairs. He noted she had her shoes on, so he wrapped her coat around her and took the keys out of the lock. He flicked on the hall light for security and sat her on the bottom step.

'I'll just check the house,' he said, crouching down to look into her eyes. She looked at him blankly, a small nod the only sign that she had heard him at all. He quickly raced around, checking the doors and windows, the hob, the oven.

'Shall I call Eric?' He shouted from the kitchen.

'No!' Dinah replied sharply. 'Don't call him.'

Gill frowned. It must be the shock. She looked at him then, her eyes watery and unfocused. 'Promise me Gill, don't call him. She wouldn't want him there.'

Gill nodded. Knowing Eric as he did, he wasn't surprised in the least. Sensitivity and tact were not his strong suits. When their friend Peter's dad fell off a ladder last Christmas, Eric had forwarded memes of hilarious falls to their Cosplay whatsapp group. Most of which were people dressed as Santa, falling off ladders and roofs. It didn't go down well with the others, but as usual Eric laughed it off.

He locked up the house and led her to the car, slipping her keys into his pocket for safekeeping. You've got me, he wanted to say. I'm here. For you both. He didn't say it though, now wasn't the time for big gestures. Being there for her was enough. The feeling in his gut told him everything he needed to know. What he did about it was something to think about later.

Thursday

Bunny's face was a picture.

'You have a date?' The cake batter fell off her wooden spoon with a thick sounding thud on the kitchen worktop. Annabel gave her a sneaky sideways glance and went to dip her finger into the blob, but her grandmother batted her away without even looking at her. 'A real date, with who?'

'A man,' Sarah retorted sassily. 'I'm not un-dateable you know.'

'I know that,' Bunny said, scooping the mixture back into the bowl from her spotless worktop and giving the bowl a good stir. 'I'm just surprised. You haven't dated for years.' She cast a glance at Annabel, a look of guilt crossing her features. 'I'll do the rest Annabel darling, you get on with your homework.' Annabel pursed her lips. Normally she wouldn't need asking twice about homework, but she sensed that this conversation was juicy, and obviously even the pull of science homework wasn't enough to quell her curiosity.

Sarah looked at her daughter, who was currently moving her head between the two women in her life like she was watching tennis. She knelt in front of her, dropping a kiss on her cheek.

'Go do your homework sweetheart, Mummy will talk to you later.'

Annabel pouted, but a pointed look from her grandmother had her trudging reluctantly upstairs.

'Mum,' Sarah said, turning back to her mother who was now scooping bun mixture into cases. 'I can't be with Greg, it doesn't work. I need to move on. If Rory can take the plunge, then so can I.'

'What's this got to do with Rory?'

'Nothing, I just...he's changing himself, coming out of his shell and trying to find a partner, and it got me thinking. I can't live like this any longer, I need to make my own life too.'

'Scared of being left behind?' Bunny asked, hitting the nail right on the head.

'No! Don't be daft!'

'You are the daft one my girl, if you think Rory meeting a lady friend will change your relationship. The man loves you to bits, he won't change that.'

'Even if he gets married, and has kids? He won't have the time to listen to me droning on, or to take Annabel shopping, not like he does. He'll have his own family to look after.'

Bunny thrust the bun trays into the oven, flicking the door shut with her slippered foot. 'Wow, the boy hasn't even had a date yet, and you've got him married off with kids already. Are you that worried? Who's this date of yours?'

'He's called Nigel, I met him on - at the club.' Sarah blushed. Letting her mother know she had signed up to a dating app was probably not the best move. The woman thought social media was a den of iniquity, which, judging from some of the profiles and dick pics she had received wasn't wide of the mark. Manscaping was evidently in though, which was good to know. Less of a shock when the time came and all that. Although, if she pulled one with a stencil design like some of the ones she had been sent, all bets were off. Lightning bolts were never sexy. Who wanted their penis to look like Harry Potter?

'Oh no, not some drunk. Sarah!' Bunny was horrified. 'Your father liked his ale, but trust me, beer farts and bad breath are not attractive in the morning. Is he a regular? What if it doesn't work out? You'll have to see him you know.'

'No, Mum, he was on a work do. He doesn't come in normally, we won't cross paths if it doesn't go well.'

He lived in Wakefield, far enough from Leeds to be worth a shot, close enough to see each other again if the first date wasn't absolutely horrendous. He looked nice, and the photos he had showed no penis or testicle candids, which was a tick in his favour. They had been chatting for a while, and no alarm bells had rung yet.

'What about Rory? Does he know?'

Sarah shook her head. 'No, I'm not going to tell him till at least the first date is over with. There probably won't be anything to tell anyway, and he's pretty busy at the moment. Sasha called the club you know, to find out about him. Luckily, I got the call - she's really annoyed that she doesn't know who and what he is. It's hilarious. As if she knows everyone in Leeds, I mean really, who does she think she is? Paris Hilton?'

Bunny didn't answer, and when Sarah looked at her, she was looking back at her with a strange expression on her features.

'What? I'm not being bitchy, I just don't really understand the attraction.'

Bunny nodded slowly, a slow smile on her lips. 'I know dear, I understand, believe me.'

Sarah shook her head at her mother, leaving the room like a sullen teenager. Living with her mother made her feel like one sometimes. The woman was acting plain weird, like she knew something Sarah didn't. She chose to focus on her date. Rory would be fine, he was a smart guy.

***

Rory was anything but fine. He was a nervous ball of energy, his hand shaking so much that the text on his phone was a big bright blur. He walked into the office he shared with Gill on shaky legs, blinking rapidly to try to get them to focus on the words. She had tried to find out about him! He felt like taking a spanner to his tap, any excuse to get that smarmy player plumber back to boast that he could pull a woman, thank you very much, even with the cardigan and lack of DIY skills. Looking down at the clothes he had on, his gloating bubble popped. She hadn't gone for the cardigan, had she? She had gone for the stranger in the VIP area, the one with the aloof attitude and the finger on the pulse. Not him. The man she liked had been more like Dad. He thought of his mother, telling him to be a good man, and pushed the thought away. Being alone wasn't enough anymore. Surely everyone changed a little?

Gill walked in then, carrying a package of fruit wrapped in brown paper under his arm. He was dressed in a dark brown suit, looking uncharacteristically smart and subdued. He looked at Rory, and both men grunted at each other distractedly.

The rest of the morning was spent drinking coffee and ignoring each other, both jumping at the sound of their mobiles pinging. When it came to lunch, they still hadn't uttered a word to each other. Pretty much like every day that week.

Rory's stomach grumbled, and as though on cue, the sandwich lady strode in from reception.

‘Lunchtime boys, we have chicken tikka today, any takers?’

Both men looked up, squinting at the light streaming in from the blinds like vampires. Brenda, who ran the local sandwich shop with her husband, tutted to herself and drew the blinds up. Gill hissed, covering his eyes.

'Dear God, you boys should really get out there and get some fresh air. It smells like a museum in here. You'll go cross eyed! Put down that work and come and get some food.' Brenda filled both guys' arms up with food and drinks and satisfied, she ruffled their hair as though they were her children, heading off with their backpacks and their packed lunches to go to school. 'You make sure you eat that, and not while you're working! Crack a window too.' She gave them a stern look and headed off to feed and mother more grey office workers.

'She has a point,' Gill said, tucking into a tuna and cucumber baguette.

Rory nodded. 'What's happening with you?' he asked, remembering his odd attire and strange package.

Gill sighed heavily. 'Dinah's mum, she's in hospital.'

Rory could have kicked himself. 'I'm sorry man, I just figured it was dating crap getting you down, like me. Is she okay? How's Dinah?'

Gill shook his head, and a haunting look invaded his expression. 'It's not good actually, they still have her on sedation for the moment. Dinah's a mess. I've been sleeping on the couch.'

Rory twigged. 'So, the suit?'

Gill laughed. 'Her dad's. I haven't wanted to leave her to get clothes.'

Rory laughed then, and Gill joined in. 'Laugh it up mate. I ran out of boxers, so I am commando in this thing.'

Rory dissolved then, lost at the thought of his mate going rough in a stranger's threads. 'Does Dinah know?' He said, between chuckles.

'No,' Gill's smile disappeared. 'She doesn't know much of anything. I dropped her at the hospital to come to work, I'm leaving early to collect her and take her home. I need to call home too. She's in a bad way - Eric keeps calling her, but she won't answer, she won't call any family. She just wants me and her mum. It's been over a week. I don't know what the deal is with her and Eric, but I feel awful. I've been blowing her calls off lately, doing our nice guys thing. I've been downright mean sometimes. The plan is over for me, Rory. I have to be there for her.'

Rory nodded. He knew that if something happened to his dad, he would be the same with Sarah, and he knew she would do the same. 'I totally understand, don't worry. Finish lunch and head off, get a shower before you see her again. You look like shit.'

Gill ran a hand through his curly hair. 'Did I mention her sofa is a two seater? I slept bolt upright in the armchair last night. I'm considering buying a blow up mattress.'

'Do they know how long she'll be in for?'

Gill shook his head. 'It's not that simple at the moment, a lot of departments are getting involved.'

Rory nodded, thinking of his mother. He didn't want to pry, and it wasn't Gill's news to share. Sick was sick in his book. The details weren't important, being there for the person was what mattered.

'Anyway,' Gill said, trying to shake off his sombre mood. 'Dating worries, eh?'

Rory shrugged. 'I'm not moaning to you about the fact that I have my dream woman chasing me, with what's on your plate.'

'It worked!' Gill threw his arms in the air, belatedly realising he had a jam donut in his hand. The jam squirted onto his borrowed suit. 'Of course,' he said, looking up at the ceiling. 'Why give me a break!?' The question went unanswered of course. Gill wiped the jam off and licked his finger. 'When's the date then?'

Rory shrugged. 'Nothing yet, she's just asking around about me. Sarah spoke to her at the club. I don't quite know what to do next. Am I even doing the right thing? The minute she speaks to me she's going to realise I'm not what I've been pretending to be. Then what?'

Gill swallowed the rest of his donut and wiped his mouth on a napkin. 'You're not a bad guy, she's going to love you. The rest of it is just to get you two together. It's not like you're a super geek or something.'

Rory nodded, wanting to believe his mate's words of advice. Gill picked up his package and saluted him. 'I'm off, going to get ready and get Dinah. I'm going to see if she wants to go out for some food tonight, take her mind off things. They end visiting hours early on the ward, to settle the patients.

'Sounds good mate, and listen, email me your schedule for tomorrow, I can cover your work for the rest of the week and rearrange what I can't. Take some time off and spend it with her.'

Gill was already shaking his head, but Rory ignored him. 'Gill, we're the bosses, we never take time off. Think about it.'

Gill hugged his business partner, and Rory patted him affectionately. 'Oh, and Rory, if my mother calls?'

Rory nodded vigorously. 'I know, avoid her whenever possible, blame work. If all else fails, you moved to Peru to be a rabbi.'

Gill looked pleased. 'That should work. If all else fails, tell her Scotty finally beamed me up.'

CHAPTER TEN

Friday

The water cooler was full. Not just of fresh water, but of gossiping bodies, feigning the need to quench their thirst so that they could quell their desire to trade stories about each other, their clients, their neighbours. PR was about presenting their best self to the world, making their world Instagram perfect, Pinterest worthy. A pimple? Airbrushed. Hairy top lip? Send a waxer in. Affair? Send in the spin doctors. Heck, sign the mistresses up. Yorkshire was less high profile than London sure, but their firm was busy enough.

'She's coming!' Someone shouted, slamming down their handset. 'She's in the foyer!'

The water cooler lost its worshippers, as pairs of heels and brogues headed for their desks as though they were undertaking their morning jog, only with the breath of the devil herself on the back of their necks. The idle chatter and laughter of the office was replaced by the tapping of keys, the sound of people dialling numbers, dealing with clients. Even the television on the wall had been changed from Jeremy Kyle to the news channel. The lift pinged, and anxious eyes risked a peek over their partition walls. Whatever came out of the lift in the next ten seconds, would determine the mood of the whole office for the remainder of the day.

The lift doors opened, and Sasha Birkenstock stepped out. Her expression was tight, closed. She spoke to no-one, heading straight for her office. Normally by now she would be screeching and shouting demands for coffee, newspapers and rolling heads, but she stayed silent. Her lips pursed as she surveyed the office, and an eerie quiet fell over the workers. This was unknown territory. Brows were waggling left and right, shoulders shrugging at each other in record numbers. What the hell was wrong with Sasha?

Walking into her office, she closed the door. Behind her, she could hear the murmurs of her co-workers, obviously relieved that there was a slab of wood between them. She knew that they would be talking about her behaviour, but she didn't care. What she did care about was the fact that the other night she had felt out of control. She didn't do that. She never lost control. It made her feel sick, but yet she wanted to know more. More about him. He was a bit of an enigma, and she wondered why he seemed so familiar, and yet so mysterious. Who the hell was he? She knew his friends didn't hang around with the usual circles of social cliques, but was this because he was in the wrong ones, or because she wasn't part of them? Was she losing her edge? She had missed out on a prime product opportunity already. Was he in PR? Was he the new her? The woman on the phone at the club had been positively snidey, as though she was in on some big joke that Sasha couldn't possibly understand. She had worked her way up this firm, using her flame red hair, big assets and exterior bravado to push her way to the top. No-one was going to keep her down ever again, that's for sure. She was on her own, and that was fine, but now she realised, some things were always going to unnerve her. What she needed to do was sort out her a-game and get back on top. She always knew her prey inside out, she knew just how to make a man putty in her hands, either for work or for a leg up, in more ways in one. This guy was outplaying her, one step ahead, and it didn't sit right with her. Her father taught her, always be one step ahead. He had missed a step and look what happened to him. She wanted no chance of history repeating itself, no way. Sasha Birkenstock always came out on top.

Crossing the carpet to her desk, she flung down her handbag and took off her coat, throwing it over the back of her office chair. Pressing a button on her phone, she buzzed through to her assistant.

'Courtney, I need coffee and breakfast. Send out for my usual and get Miranda's on the line.'

Courtney simpered down the line at her. 'Yeah Courtney, just do it. I don't need your life story.' She slammed down the phone, and it rang back seconds later, signifying her outgoing call had been placed. She smiled to herself, settling in behind her desk. Sasha was back.

'Doug, hi! Sasha here.'

Greg slunk out of work, gym bag on his shoulder. He had just had the world's most boring set of shifts and was pretty much cursing his parents for letting him stay up late as a kid to watch London's Burning and The Bill. Working in the fire service always looked so interesting, so epic. If they had seen him cleaning gunk out of pipes and doing laundry and cooking the last few days, the women who dreamed of a hot man sliding down a pole might just pop their fantasy bubble. He was looking forward to a good work out at the gym. Sarah had been avoiding his calls for days, only sending the odd text when he enquired about Annabel. He knew that she was pulling away from him, he just didn't know why. Maybe cancelling the last few visiting times hadn't helped, but Bunny was there to help. A man had the right to work, and he did help with the money side of things. Although, he hadn't really seen them to hand over any cash. Maybe that was it. He pulled his phone out of his bag as he walked to the gym that was round the corner from the station. Pulling up his texts, he saw she hadn't replied to his last text, asking if she was working that night. She did different nights - she should tell him what nights they were! He had a right to know where the mother of his child was at all times. She had never understood or liked that, but it wasn't about what she wanted. She had his child, which linked them together forever. It didn't matter what she thought, and he fully intended to make her see that one day. Just thinking about it was making him mad. He walked up the gym steps, tapping away on his phone.

I TEXTED YOU, GOT NO REPLY. ARE YOU WORKING TONIGHT? WAS GOING TO COME AND SEE ANNABEL. TEXT ME BACK.

He sent it and before he had a chance to cross the foyer, it beeped back.

CAN'T DO TONIGHT, SORRY. WORKING. WILL ARRANGE ANOTHER NIGHT.

That was it? Short and blunt. When a woman texted you like that, she was mad. It was the equivalent of her saying 'nothing's wrong, I'm fine' in person. When a woman said that, you knew to hit the floor, kiss the ground and hope for the best. Sarah wasn't often like this, she tended to get on with it. That's one of the things that attracted him to her in the first place. She wasn't needy like the others, he could leave her to her own devices and she would cope.

He headed to the locker room, saying hello to a few regulars he recognised. He stopped just outside the changing rooms and dialled. He cringed when he heard the answering voice.

'Bunny, it's Greg. Sarah there?'

Bunny positively growled down the phone. ‘Hello to you too, Gregory.’ She knew he hated his full name, so of course she used it at every opportunity. ‘She's not in.’

Greg pinched the bridge of his nose between his fingers, resisting the urge to punch the wall. ‘So, where is she? At college? Is she working tonight?’

Bunny hesitated, and Greg's eyes narrowed. ‘Gregory, she may live with me, but I am not her secretary, or her keeper.’ He could hear Annabel laughing in the background, some show's theme music blaring out. ‘And, for the record,’ she added, lowering her voice, ‘neither are you. Let us know when you want to see your daughter again.’ The line went dead, and Greg looked at the screen dumbly. She hung up on him? Since when?

Greg pushed through the locker room doors, fixing a fake easy smile on his face. Inside, he was raging. Absolutely raging at the audacity of the old bag. Sarah moving in with her had been a massive mistake. It was much better when they had first met. She had her own flat; he could come and go as he pleased, Sarah was easier going, used to her own single carefree life. She worked less. Cracked a smile now and then. He missed that Sarah. Since she got pregnant with Annabel and gave up the flat to save money, things had changed, and not all for the better. Living with the mother for example. Now he had to book an appointment to go see his daughter. He didn't like the changes. It was time to do something about it too.

***

Friday night, and Rory was excited for the weekend. After a full week of work, dealing with both his and Gill's clients, he was more than ready for a break. He wanted to deal with the paperwork at Miranda's, head home and chill out in front of the television. Doug however, seemed to have other ideas. The minute he walked into the club, Doug appeared in the foyer.

'Dad?' Rory said in surprise, as he signed the visitors log. 'What's wrong?'

Doug was dressed in his smartest threads - one of his favourite suits - matching with a white dress shirt and tie. 'Nothing's wrong son, I rang the office, left a message.'

Rory nodded. 'Sorry Dad, I'm covering the office on my own for now, so things have been a bit hectic. Time of year and all that, tax season. You got a date?'

Doug looked confused, and Rory pointed at his clothes as they both started to walk through the main doors. 'The suit, pretty flash. Not seen that one in a while.'

Doug flushed, grinning at him. 'I actually thought that we could go out, have dinner together. There's something we need to talk about.'

Rory stiffened. 'Tonight? Could we not do it another time?'

Doug's face fell, and Rory felt a pang of guilt. 'Son, I just want to have dinner with you, to talk. Could you not spare the time?'

Rory sighed, looking around at the mostly empty club. 'Okay Dad, fine. I'll come to dinner.'

Doug seemed to grow in stature before his son, and Rory thought of his mother. What would she make of their relationship now? Perhaps a dinner wouldn't be the end of the world.

'Great, ten minutes, out the front? We'll take a taxi, have a drink.'

Rory nodded, walking to the office to put his briefcase away. He could come back tomorrow to do the paperwork. A drink might be a good thing.

Sarah pulled up to work an hour after Rory and Doug had left in a taxi, heading for a very swanky and probably uncomfortable meal out. She parked the car in her usual spot and jumped when her mobile rang yet again. She knew without looking it was Greg. She had a separate ring tone just for him, so she could blow off his calls now without worrying about missing a call about Annabel. She had finally taken the plunge and started dating, and she wanted to get used to it herself first before anything got back to Greg and spoiled it. He wasn't going to take it well. In a selfish way, she had been glad that he had been doing his usual crappy dead beat dad routine lately. Having Annabel lie to her father wasn't something she wanted to do, but what was the alternative? She needed to move on, and she had a feeling that Greg wasn't going to like it. Did he ever like her asserting her independence? The call rang off, and immediately rang again. She banged her forehead on the steering wheel in frustration. He had been calling on and off all afternoon, and she knew he had called the house too. He didn't ask to speak to Annabel, or even ask about his daughter at all. His payments had stopped altogether too, and Sarah was definitely feeling the pinch. Even his measly contribution helped with uniforms, shoes, petrol etc. At this rate, Sarah would have to pick up extra shifts at the club, and she didn't see Annabel enough already. Not for the first time, she wished she had never set eyes on him.

Heading into the club, she remembered her words as they came screaming back into her head. Leaning against the bar - her bar - was Greg. He was dressed in a nice shirt and his best shit-eating grin. He pointed to the phone that was still in her hand and waggled his at her from across the room. Sarah stopped still, looking back at him in shock. He never came here. How did he even know what time she was coming in? She turned away, heading from the locker rooms on shaky legs, trying to quieten down the voice inside her head that told her something had changed. She had a feeling she wasn't going to like it. What a bitch! Greg cursed under his breath, pushing his phone into his pocket and motioning for another beer. She waltzed in here, phone in hand, obviously ignoring his calls. If she wasn't calling him, he wondered just who she was calling.

'And she believed it!?' Doug asked, wiping the tears from his eyes. Rory dabbed at his with a napkin, taking a large slug of wine between ripples of laughter. 'That's quite the caper.'

Rory nodded. 'I felt a bit bad, but we got rid of all of the stock we needed to, so it's a bonus.'

Doug slapped the table, making the couple at the next table jump. They were in a nice hotel restaurant not far from the city centre, all white marble steps, valets and doormen. The kind of place Doug loved to eat, the ones where there were no prices on the menus. As if knowing how much your bill would be was vulgar somehow. It drove him mad as a boy, when all he wanted was to hang out at the local burger bar with his mates or get a drive-thru. His dad said that the Merc wouldn't fit into a drive-thru. First world problems and missing mothers. That was his childhood.

'So, what's this plan you've been murmuring about? You and Gill in it together?'

Rory shook his head. 'Er, no - Gill is busy with Dinah, his friend. Her mum is sick.'

Doug nodded. 'That's good - that's he's there for her, I mean. Doesn't she have anyone?'

Rory thought of Eric. The handful of times he had met him had been enough to judge his character. 'No, not like Gill. He'll look after her.'

Doug nodded. 'So just you then? Being a man about town?'

Rory laughed awkwardly. 'Kind of. It's more trying something new, different.'

Doug sucked the air in through his teeth, studying him for a moment. 'Different isn't always good though son, don't forget to be yourself. It's all well and good playing the big man, but will you be happy with the results of this plan? If you're not being yourself, how long can you keep that up?'

'I don't know Dad, to be honest. I just know that being me isn't working. I'm still alone, rattling around every night in my house, a house I bought to eventually raise a family in. Life's short - I have to try, surely?'

His dad looked at him and nodded, ever so slowly. 'Just be careful son, don't end up like me. I can't have a relationship with the women I date, and let me tell you, that's pretty lonely too.'

Rory nodded, feeling suddenly awkward about their heart to heart. Dad was lonely. He never even mentioned that before, not even right after Mum passed. Rory had never considered that either. 'I'll be careful. Can we change the subject?'

Doug nodded, motioning to the waiter to refill his glass, and raised his eyebrows in question at his son. Rory nodded assent to the server and smiled at his dad. It had been quite nice tonight, he had to say. All awkward talk over with, they had got on better than they had in months. Years, truth be told. Rory found himself wishing that his mother was there to see it, and he looked at the empty chair.

'Me too son,' Doug said, 'I miss her too.'

'Do you think she would have been happy to see us here, like this?' He asked.

Doug didn't answer for a moment, sitting back in his seat and cradling his wine glass. 'Your mother always loved nothing more than having us with her. She lived for the times when all three of us were sat round a table, eating, talking about our day.' He winced, as though recalling the memory caused him physical pain. 'I never appreciated her while she was here, not like I should have, and I will regret it forever. I want you to know that, son.'

Rory didn't reply. He looked around and marvelled to himself how his father had suddenly opened up like this. He felt like this was a milestone for them, and he didn't want to break the spell. The diners around him were oblivious to this monumental event. They were missing the bonding between a grown father and son, eating their fine food, laughing, making plans, falling in love, creating an ending. It was all here, life in all its glory.

'So, you got me tipsy on wine to tell me that or was there something else?' He regretted his harsh words as soon as he spoke them. It was habit he realised, and it needed to stop. 'I mean, I've enjoyed it of course…but I thought you wanted to talk about something else.'

'I did son, I wanted to tell you that I'm taking a step back. I wanted to talk about you taking over a bit more, give your old man some more time to kick back his heels and do something other than work. I want to know if you want the family business.'

Rory said nothing for a long beat, taking thc bottle of wine out from its bucket and pouring them both another glass. 'Are you sick?' He asked, suddenly terrified of hearing the answer.

Doug chuckled. 'I love how you assume I have to be sick to take some time off!' He chuckled again, a deep throaty gurgle. 'I realised something the other day, that's all. I was at home, and I felt ill.'

'You are sick.' Rory stated. 'Have you been to see someone? Do you want me to come with you?'

Doug leaned forward and put his hand over Rory's. 'I'm not sick. I had the flu, that's all. I didn't ring you because I was fine. I got some medicine delivered, I ordered in, watched TV. I had a few thousand box sets to watch, been meaning to watch them for ages, so I did that.'

Rory said nothing, thinking of a time a week ago when his dad had been unusually quiet. He hadn't thought much of it, figured he was holed up somewhere with his latest Mensa candidate. He remembered being grateful even, for the break in his father's attempts to bond with him.

'The truth is, being sick was a wake up call for me…and I really enjoyed being home. Do you know some rooms, I don't even use? That house was loved so much by your mother, and I just couldn't bear to part with it when you left home, but I'm like a ghost in that place. I don't really even live there, it's just somewhere I sleep. So, I slept in, watched TV, cooked. Aside from the fact I was ill, it was pretty good. What I did notice though, was that aside from work purposes, no-one called me.' He put his hand up to stop his son from interrupting. 'I'm not having a go, you have your own life, and God knows I haven't always been there. I just realised, that if I don't sort out my future now, I am going to die a very rich, very lonely old man in a huge house full of memories from the past. So, I'm going to retire, and I'm going to start dating.'

Rory opened his mouth to speak, but Doug pointed a finger at him. 'I know, I know, I never stopped dating. I mean properly, with a woman my own age, who wants to be with someone properly, and not for the money and status.'

'I think that's great Dad, but I don't know about work, I'm not sure about how we can sort it out.'

'I know, and you have your own business, no need for any of my businesses - take the club, for now. Give me one month, come and work in the club. Be the manager, run the promotions. You can bring your work to the office, work from here if you like. Once Gill's back of course. We can get you an assistant, ask Sarah if she wants more hours maybe. Whatever you need.' He motioned for the bill and sighed deeply. 'I feel so much better now, getting that off my chest. Your car's at the club, you can't drive now so fancy coming back with me for one? See what you would be running?'

Rory looked at his father and made a decision. He really needed to change, and maybe if he was changing the way he dealt with the women in his life, he should work on the relationships with the male counterparts of his life a different way too.

'Okay,' Rory said, and Doug's head snapped back in surprise.

'Wow, I should get you drunk more often, if this is how I get you to talk.' Doug paid the bill and the two men headed to the reception.

'I think we both need a change of scene, Dad.' Rory said, feeling rosy from the wine. He put his arm around his father, giving him a squeeze. He felt thin, diminished somehow under the fabric of the suit. He squeezed him again, resolving to make the most of their time together. Sarah had told him for years to make it up with his father, but this was the first time that Rory had even considered it.

'Is he bothering you?' Frankie asked, pointing her head at the man at the end of the bar. Sarah shook her head.

'No, it's fine.' She finished making her drinks on the back of the bar, putting them all on a tray. 'Thanks though.'

Frankie pouted, her bright magenta lipstick looking all the brighter under the lights of the club. 'The guy has stalker written all over him. Don't go for a break alone, okay?'

Sarah nodded, and Frankie squeezed her on the shoulder and got back to work. Sarah flicked her gaze across to him. He was watching her, and their eyes locked. He smiled, just a hint of a smile, and raised one brow. Sarah's blood chilled. He was angry. She knew it, could almost see his anger bubbling away under the surface of his easy gait. She had pissed him off. Good, she thought. Good.

She kept working, making a point not to look at him again. Staying at the opposite end of the bar, she winked at Frankie, who had taken it on herself to serve him without a word.

'So,' Greg shout-slurred, 'I haven't seen you before.' Frankie

rolled her eyes, snatching the note from his hand.
'Wow, original. I haven't seen you before, so what?' She operated the till, dumping the change on the bar instead of in his hand.

Greg laughed. 'Whoo hoo, you're a fiery one, I like that.'

Frankie snorted, moving on to a group of girls who came to the bar. Greg's face darkened, and Sarah blew the air out through her cheeks. Greg was drunk, and it wasn't even ten o'clock. Tonight wasn't going to be a lot of fun. She looked around the club, seeing who else was on that night. Maybe she could try and get an early finish, sneak off home out of the way. It had to be worth a shot. She went to the end of the bar into the wash room and dialled the office on the land line screwed to the wall. No answer. Sarah huffed and put the phone down.

'You looking for the boss? He went out a few hours ago, said he would be back late but was taking the night off.' Alex was in the wash room, stacking glasses of all different sizes into the dishwasher.

'Great. Who's in charge then?'

Alex shrugged. 'I thought you were?'

Sarah picked up the phone and dialled reception. 'Winston? It's me. Where's Doug? Well, is he coming in? Who's Duty Manager?' Winston's reply made Alex wince, as he watched Sarah's face fall. 'Rick's on?' Rick was the manager who ran the day to day minutiae of the club, but Doug always worked weekend nights. For him to go out and not tell anyone was unheard of. Rick was fine, but he wasn't someone to confide in. He didn't know about Greg, no-one did.

'Okay, will you ask Rick to come and see me when he gets a minute, I need an early finish if any come up.' She didn't wait for an answer, putting the phone down and pushing through the doors back to the bar. They were busy, and she had left Frankie alone.

'You want to lose your hand?' She heard Frankie shout as she walked back through the door. Looking across, she saw Frankie reach forward and peel Greg's hand off hers with her free one. 'Do not touch me again.' She reached under the bar and pressed the panic button for security. Sarah raced to her side, and she could see three doormen running towards the bar. Pressing that button meant trouble, come running. Greg was shouting at Frankie, grabbing her other hand tight. Frankie was punching his hand to get him off. Sarah launched herself on top of the bottle fridge, landing on her knees. She slammed her hands into Greg's chest, shoving him with all her might.

'Get off her!' She bellowed. Greg, drunk and surprised, lost his balance and flew backwards, straight into the arms of the bouncers.

He looked at her with a mixture of shock and pure anger. 'What the fuck are you doing?' He screamed. 'How dare you!'

Sarah, still kneeling on the fridge, jabbed her finger at him. 'Something I should have done a long time ago, Greg! Push back!'

The bouncers bundled him off, kicking and screaming out of the door. Frankie hugged Sarah to her. 'Thanks mate, that was awesome!'

Sarah hugged her back, pulling away to check her arms. 'You okay?' She searched for injuries frantically. Her arms were red, and she could see the beginnings of fingerprints forming. Her breath caught in her throat, a sob bubbling up.

'I'm so sorry, Frankie.' She hugged her friend to her, ignoring the crowd of people who were now watching them. 'I'm so sorry.'

Frankie squeezed her back. 'Hey, don't be daft! You saved me from some weirdo drunk, it was pretty intense. Have you met him before, you said his name?'

Sarah sobbed again. 'He's Annabel's dad.'

Frankie's eyes widened, but she said nothing. 'You were amazing, so thank you. Now go clean yourself up, get a coffee. I'll get Alex to come and give me a hand till you get back.'

Sarah went to decline the offer but started crying again. This was bad. She needed to call her mother, warn her in case he showed up. She headed to the locker room, ignoring the stares of the revellers around her.

***

Greg was furious, swearing and staggering around outside the main doors of the club. Two of the bouncers were holding him back from the doors, keeping him separated from the customers still coming in. Friday nights were busy, and not even a drunken, angry man would put anyone off coming in to party.

'My girlfriend is in there, you can't just throw me out!' Greg ranted, pointing at the doors. 'I'm a fireman you know, I save people's lives. All I wanted was to see my girlfriend, and to have a drink. That a crime? That barmaid was hitting on me. You should really think about who you employ. Employing sluts is all well and good but -'

'Hey,' Winston shouted from behind the glass, making everyone jump around him. 'Do not call our girls that name, that's not true. You have two minutes to leave, before we call the police. Nathan, get him the hell away from my door.'

Greg gave him the finger, laughing drunkenly. 'Sit on it, I ain't going anywhere. Call the cops. Tell them I said hi, I work with half of them. And tell my girlfriend I want her to come out here, now.'

Winston's jaw clenched. 'Which poor girl is stupid enough to date you?'

'Sarah Jennings, tell her to get her ass out here.'

'Winston, don't tell Sarah anything,' a strong voice came from behind Greg. He spun around clumsily, trying to throw off the bouncers that were holding him up. Rory stood there, eyes set hard on Greg, his dad next to him sporting much the same expression.

'Rory! What the hell are you doing here?' Greg sang. His glazed eyes flicked to Doug. 'Oh,' he snorted, pointing a shaky finger. 'I remember, daddy dearest eh? Must be nice, having a rich little daddy. Some of us have to work for a living.'

Rory said nothing, smiling at Greg calmly. 'Dad, you go in, check in with Rick, I'll be in in a minute.'

'No, I don't think -'

'Dad,' Rory said again firmly. 'I need you to go and check on things.'

Doug nodded, patting his son on the shoulder. 'I'll get the round in.' He looked at Greg pointedly. 'With my huge piles of money. I work too son, and you are now barred from this club. Have a good night.' He nodded to the bouncers and Winston and walked through the main doors. Greg watched him go, his lip curled, stained from the shots he must have been slinging back.

'Greg, it's time to leave now. You can speak to Sarah tomorrow, when you've sobered up.'

Greg went to move forward, and Rory motioned for the bouncers to let him go. He came closer and Rory's nose wrinkled at the overpowering smell of alcohol.

'I came to see Sarah. She's ignoring me, and I won't be

ignored. Let me in so I can talk to her.'

Rory shook his head, and Greg poked him hard in the chest.

'You think you're hot shit don't you, Rory?' He said Rory like a child would, teasing, singsong and baby like. 'This has nothing to do with you. Get Sarah out here, cos I ain't leaving.'

Rory looked at Winston. 'If he doesn't leave in the next two minutes, call the police. Nathan, Phil - keep him out please.' The two bouncers nodded and came forward to steer him away.

'Jesus, I can't even talk to my girlfriend now? You guys are ridiculous.'

'She's not your girlfriend Greg. Was she ever, really?'

Greg's face darkened, his eyes almost black, shark-like. 'Jealous, are we? I doubt she would sleep with you, but you could always ask. She's not bad either.'

Greg never saw it coming. He was out cold, flat on his back before anyone had the chance to blink. Everyone stood stunned momentarily, staring at Greg laid spark out on the floor. Winston chuckled, a low deep rumble, and it broke the spell. The bouncers went to check on Greg, and Rory stood there, flexing his hand open and closed.

'Get him out of here,' he growled. He walked through the club, heading for the office. He was so mad, so angry. He wanted to go back and smash Greg's stupid face in. He wanted to punish him for speaking like that about someone he cared about. He headed straight for Sarah's bar but saw she wasn't there.

'Frankie, where's Sarah?' He shouted over the noise.

'Break room,' she shouted back, pulling an apologetic face. Rory nodded his thanks.

'He's gone, don't worry. He won't get back in.' Frankie looked relieved and headed back to the crowd of baying punters. The club was in full swing now, and Rory couldn't help but look at it differently, after his father's words. He always hated this place, but the reasons why eluded him now. It was a business after all, why did he hate it so much?

Looking into the staff room, he couldn't see Sarah, so he headed to the office. Doug was just passing her a whisky tumbler. The ice jangled in her glass, as her hands shook. They both looked to the door as he arrived. Sarah looked awful, tearful and sobbing.

'Rory, I'm so sorry. I need to call Mum, she has Annabel. He might come to the house.'

Rory went to sit next to her, and she dissolved into floods of tears again when he put his arm around her. Doug bent down to his knees in front of him. Both men sober now, concern and adrenaline burning off the alcohol.

'I'll go to Bunny's now and stay with them both. He won't come round - and even if he does, he won't get past the front gate.'

Rory looked at his dad in shock. His father seemed to be full of surprises these days. 'You sure, Dad?' Doug was already on his way out, shrugging his coat on.

'Of course I am, Rick can handle things here.'

'Thanks,' he said and stood to hug his dad. 'I appreciate it.'

'No problem. Nice left hook,' he murmured, nodding towards the monitor. Rory covered his knuckles. Doug hugged him, dropping a kiss onto Sarah's forehead before he left. She had stopped crying now and was sat staring into space.

'It's my fault. I've been ignoring him. He came to talk to me,

I think, and got drunk. He hurt Frankie...' She started to sob again, her voice breaking. 'I just saw red. Did I hurt him?'

Rory shook his head. 'None of this is your fault, and he seemed fine to me. What happened?'

'He had hold of her. He was hurting her so I just shoved him, to get him off her. I had to get him off.'

Rory raised his eyebrows but said nothing. 'That must have taken a lot. I'm glad you did it.'

She blew her nose. 'I wish I hadn't. It's going to make things so tricky now, he's just going to cause problems.'

'You don't have to take it Sar, get a solicitor - get something formal in place.'

'He would hate that! He isn't paying me either, hasn't for a while, I really can't afford it.'

Rory headed over to the ice bucket, filling one of the clean cotton hankies from his dad's desk drawer with ice. 'I can help, I have a solicitor friend.'

'No Rory, I can't do that. What's the ice for?' Her gaze dropped to his hand. 'What the hell happened?'

Rory winced as he put the ice onto his sore knuckles. 'I punched Greg. I knocked him out.' Sarah's mouth dropped. 'I know, I know. I'm really sorry, he just got into my head, he said something, and I just lost my temper.'

Sarah dropped her head into her hands, and her shoulders started to shake. Rory cursed himself, but then he heard her laugh. It started as a titter, and then turned into hysterical laughter.

'You punched Greg! I - I can't believe it. I...just can't believe you did that!'

Rory started to laugh with her. 'I can't really believe it either. I thought Winston was going to wet himself. The bouncers think I've flipped my lid.'

Sarah snorted, and Rory went to sit on the couch next to her, bringing a tumbler of whisky with him. They clinked their glasses together. Sarah dried her tears with the back of her hand.

'Here's to moving forward,' Rory said. 'Call the solicitor, get out from under this.'

'I'll think about it. Where were you, anyway?'

'Dad wants to retire, he wants me to take over.'

They both sat back, Sarah's head tucked into his shoulder. Rory rested his cheek on top of her head. They both drained their glass.

'What a night.' Sarah said.

'Yep,' he agreed, pulling her closer. He was so glad she was okay, and that he was there. Maybe working at the club would work out for the best, for now at least.

'Hey, I might just have some work for you here,' he said, and she looked up at him. 'Just in the office, with me.'

'Okay,' she said, squeezing his hand. 'You can make your own damn coffee though.'

They both laughed and got another drink.

CHAPTER ELEVEN

Sunday

Rory walked into the restaurant, smiling at the doorman and trying his hardest not to look around frantically for her. He was every inch the normal Rory on the exterior; calm, collected. He had on his new dress shirt, new slacks picked by Doug. The pair of them had been shopping, got lunch and talked. It was weird, an odd sensation to be doing things with the man who had supposedly raised him. Things they never did when he was growing up. He was actually quite sad to miss their Sunday tea for this meal in a way, but Doug had understood. He still didn't agree with the plan, he could tell, but he was going along with it.

It was still an adjustment. Sometimes Rory had to bite his tongue when they chatted, years of resentment threatening to spill out. Memories were evoked from the simplest things; the memory of a meal in a restaurant they passed. His mum seemed to walk beside them sometimes…Rory felt as though he could feel her there. He wondered if his father felt her too. One day, he might even get the bottle to ask him about those last days. When they were both strong enough to open that box. He walked to the pedestal, where a smartly dressed woman was just finishing a phone call.

'Good evening,' she said brightly, dazzling Rory with her stunning mega kilo watt smile. 'Do you have a reservation? Ah…Mr Gallant, your table is ready, but your guest hasn't arrived yet. Would you like to take your seat or get a drink at the bar?'

Rory smiled in return. 'I'll take the table please, and can you send the wine list over?'

'Of course,' the lady moved her hand to her side, like a model on a game show, and Rory followed her, taking a seat at a discreet table for two in the corner. His dad had booked it, and he knew it was one of the best tables in the house. He felt wary about the date. It felt a bit like they had been set up for a date, rather than her calling him up at the club. She had left a message, but then arrangements had been made with her assistant. They hadn't spoken on the phone to each other, it was madness.

Sarah had stepped in to act as his assistant, much to Rory's reluctance. 'She's getting the upper hand, don't you see? Trying to make you chase her a bit. You need to keep it up, if you really want her. It's working.'

So here he was, having a Sunday evening meal. Not the best night for a hot date, another one of Sarah's ideas. After all, a busy man about town was busy on the trendier nights, right? He thought of his usual Sunday evenings, coming home after an awkward meal with his dad, ironing his shirts in front of the TV, paying his bills. All he needed was a pipe and slippers and he was done. He wouldn't be telling Sasha that of course, he couldn't imagine her spending many nights like that. Maybe after this they could spend more together.

He took a seat at the table, pouring himself a glass of water, concentrating on stopping his hand shaking the ice right out of the jug. He was just raising the glass to his lips when the server came back over. Rory stood quickly and almost legged himself up on his chair.

'Mr Gallant, your guest is here.'

'Thank you.' She left, and there stood Sasha. She looked amazing, dressed in a tight fitting red dress that shone and sparkled in the tastefully dimmed lighting of the restaurant. Several diners had obviously turned to witness her arrival, something Rory was suddenly sorry he'd missed.

'Hi there,' she said, giving him a friendly little wave of her fingers.

'Hi!' He squeaked, moving around the table to pull out her chair. 'Sit down, please.'

She shimmied into the chair, and Rory pushed it gently into the table. Taking his own seat, he tried his best to look relaxed. A little slouchy, but apparently that was how 'real men' sat. Sarah had even made a joke about him sitting with his legs wide open, like blokes seemed to do on trains, buses, the couch. Rory had laughed at the time, but now it was all he saw. Why did they do that? He had the same equipment as them, and he had never felt like he needed to give them more air or sit with his hands down his pants to check that they were there, for that matter. His dad never did it, and other than the odd codpiece Gill sported in his many costumes, he kept his junk to himself too. Was it a generational thing?

'Rory?' He looked up, realising that Sasha was looking at him quizzically. He had his dream date finally sat in front of him, looking like she was drawn by angels, and he was sitting here thinking about Gill's penis. Not the best start, was it?

'Sorry,' he said, recovering as best he could. He gave her his best smile (one of his new ones, he had practised those too) and slouched a little lower in his chair. 'I'm glad you're here. You look beautiful, by the way.' Nice recovery, Gallant.

She looked down at herself momentarily. ‘I know, right? New client, they make the best clothes.’ She moved her manicured and long nailed hands down the sides of her dress, running her palms along her breasts and down her rib cage. ‘It feels like pure silk, which of course it is.’

Rory saw a couple sat just to the side of them watch her movements. The man in particular, till his date leant forward and slapped his hand. He looked away, throwing a guilty look back at Rory. The wine waiter came then with the wine list, and Rory busied himself with looking at the choices to collect himself. Her confidence had unnerved him up close. He didn't want his mask to slip. Modesty didn't always go hand in hand with confidence, after all. That was fine. She was in PR.

‘So,’ she said, when the wine had been poured and they had been left with the menus, ‘we finally meet. I feel like I know you from somewhere though, and I know a lot of people.’

Rory nodded. ‘We might have crossed paths, I go to a lot of events. You work in PR or something, right?’

Her face fell a little. ‘Actually, I'm the head of PR for my firm. I have quite a portfolio of clients.’ She pushed her nose a little in the air, and Rory felt a pang of guilt. He knew full well what she did, he had stalked her social media accounts for weeks, checking out her firm and the work she did. He wanted to apologise but wasn't it the point, being nonchalant and aloof? It had got him this far, surely he should keep it up. He didn't need to be a complete jerk though. Tonight was going to be an education.

‘Sounds great,’ he said, taking a sip of wine. ‘Tell me more about it.’

***

'This is delicious,' she purred, spooning another piece of chocolate tarte into her mouth. 'How's yours?' Dinner had got better, thankfully. Whether it was the fact that they had drank the best part of two bottles of wine, or that they had relaxed into each other remained to be seen. There had been a few awkward moments, sure, like when she asked about his work, and when she had insisted on taking photos of every course and posting them online. Rory had never quite got that, why people took photographs of the plates of food they were about to eat. When did this become a thing? Chefs, sure - cookbooks always had photographs of the food in them, the finished product and the stages of cooking. That was expected, but why did the average person take photos? What was next, taking a snap of the poop it produced? Instacrap? Rory shuddered at the thought. She didn't take a picture of anything but the food, the candles on the table, so perhaps it was a work thing. He took it in his stride, acting as though it was perfectly normal. It was her world, and he wanted to be a part of it. She was talking about herself a lot, sure, but who didn't on a date?' It was basically a job interview, for the longest job ever.

'It's pretty amazing actually, I'm just sorry I'm still full from the beef.'

She giggled, and he noticed how natural her laugh sounded. It sounded so different to when he heard it in the club. Maybe she was actually enjoying herself. 'Do you fancy coffee or maybe a drink elsewhere?' she asked, looking straight at him as she dabbed her mouth with a napkin. The man on the next table looked like he wanted to be that napkin. His date looked like he wanted to strangle Sasha with it. He was about to snatch her hand off at the invitation but then remembered one of the dating rules. Leave them wanting more. He gave her his best apologetic smile. 'I'm sorry, I have a busy day tomorrow, raincheck?'

Sasha was prevented from answering by a loud bang at the side of them. Rory looked across, and he could see that the nosy diner was lifting his hand off the table, as though he'd slammed it down. Sasha was busy touching up her lipstick in the mirror, so Rory mouthed 'what?' at him. The man mouthed 'idiot' back at him and was promptly hit in the face with a lemon. To be specific, a slice of lemon, ice and the remnants of his dinner date's drink.

'You really are a shithead, Anthony!' She screamed at him, smacking him with her handbag before flouncing off to the exit. The flustered, and now very wet, diner threw Rory and Sasha one last yearnful look before throwing some notes on the table and running after her.

'Wait, don't go baby! I'm sorry!'

The diners all sat in stunned silence. Sasha snapped closed her compact and smiled at him, oblivious.

'So, walk me to a taxi?'

CHAPTER TWELVE

Monday

'No way!' Sarah said, open mouthed. 'That did not happen!'

Rory chuckled, glancing at the CCTV where Winston was taking entrance fees from a group of men dressed as cowboys, some with pretty tight fitting chaps. Did they not feel the cold? 'It really did, God's honest. Seriously, when we got outside the restaurant he was on his knees and she was telling him it was over. The man was crying and everything. I felt sorry for him, to be honest. I think the plan was to propose before he got distracted.'

Sarah rolled her eyes. 'She probably dodged a bullet. They both did. How did the end of the night go? Was Sasha upset?'

'That was the funny thing. I don't think she even noticed. She didn't even look their way at all. She never said a word. We just said goodbye, I said I would call her, and she left.'

'No goodnight kisses?' She puckered her lips till she looked like a duck, making sucking noises.

'Lovely. And no, we didn't, I just put her in the car. Playing it cool, remember? I didn't feel like she wanted me to. It felt a bit like a job interview, not a date.'

Sarah pushed an invoice into a file and put it back in the cabinet. 'Of course it did, that's what a first date is. How old are you, what do you do, are you a serial killer, do you pick your feet? We all want to know what's wrong with the people we're spending the night with. The question is, do you like her?'

Rory pushed his chair back under his desk. Sarah was sat at his father's. They had spent half the week going through the invoices, seeing what cost savings they could make before they started to plan some summer events. He wanted to show his father that he could make a go of the club, even though he hadn't decided whether or not he really wanted it. Gill was still AWOL, spending every spare minute with Dinah, taking her to the hospital, staying over. His nice guy hat was definitely back on. It must be bad for her mother to still be in hospital, but Rory didn't want to ask. He and Gill had no secrets, which meant that this wasn't his secret to tell. That was Gill all over, loyal to the last.

'Of course I like her, otherwise I wouldn't be going to all this trouble. I'm just not sure she liked me, really. We got on, but I don't know if we sparked. I mean, she did of course. She sparked with half the restaurant, but I'm not sure I really wowed her. I think she's a bit...'

'Self-obsessed? Vapid?' Sarah ventured. 'Shallow? Vain?'

'Er...' Rory thought of the arguing couple outside. Even the taxi driver was nearly in tears, yet Sasha had acted as if nothing had happened. Had she even seen them? 'Nooo...I don't think it's that.'

'Wow,' Sarah said, her head now resting on her palms as she leant on the desk. Her eyelids fluttered and closed for a minute. 'You took so long to deny that I almost died. What was it then?'

Rory rubbed his fingers down his stubbly cheek. He had been working lates all week, days at the accounting firm and then nights here, and he was feeling a bit whacked. Sarah had agreed to help him, which was brilliant, but it was still a lot to take on.

'You know what, it's just me. I've thought about a date with

Sasha for so long, that I built it up in my head. First dates are hard, aren't they? That's all it is. I already rang her, and she invited me to a boxing match – one of her clients - at the weekend. I didn't even need to ask her out again, so that's a good sign right, that the plan's working?'

Sarah nodded slowly. 'Sure is. Did you tell her you think boxing is barbaric and superficial showboating, or are you leaving that till the night?'

Rory groaned. 'Give me a break, I'm supposed to be a big butch man of the world, remember? How's Belle, anyway? I miss her. What are you doing on Saturday?'

Sarah lit up, as she always did when her daughter was mentioned. 'She's good, happier even. To be honest, I think she's relieved not to have to see Greg. She's free on Saturday, no plans yet. Come over. Mum's keen on doing some pottery class or other all of a sudden, so she's going to be out a bit more.' Her face clouded. 'I think she's a bit wary of being alone in the house to be honest. She never seems to be in lately if she doesn't have Annabel. He hasn't called or anything. It's weird, Ror, he never stays away like this. I should feel relaxed, glad he's gone, but I feel like he's up to something.'

Rory put down his papers, glancing at his knuckles which still bore a couple of scratches from their impact on Greg's face. 'He won't come round, and if he does, you don't have to see him. Just call the police. He assaulted your friend, Frankie will back you up.'

Sarah shook her head. 'I can't do that. He might lose his job, and he's still Annabel's father. I can't destroy his life like that. Besides, he might tell them about you.'

'You wouldn't be destroying anything, he did that on his own.

And let him call the police on me. I'm not scared of him.'

'Rory,' Sarah was focused on her work now, not looking at him. 'Please, just leave it, okay?'

'Okay. Saturday, what are you doing?'

Sarah narrowed her eyes suspiciously. 'I have Annabel and then I'm here. Why?'

Rory clicked on the search engine on his computer. 'Don't make plans. I think we might just have a date with a rhino.'

***

Friday

Gill woke up on Friday morning feeling like he had been tied in a knot. Elaine's sofa was a two seater affair with wooden arms and legs, which meant that the fabric covering wasn't as comfortable as the more modern sofas. He gingerly straightened out his legs, wincing at the pops and cracks his bones produced. His left arm, which lay underneath him, was completely numb and he rubbed at it with the other. He rolled off the sofa as slowly as he could, hearing the sound of his back crack and his muscles moan. He would have to sleep on the floor tonight, another night on this couch and he was done for. The landline on the hall table started to ring, and Gill groaned. Eric, again. He looked at his watch, rolling his neck around in a circle to straighten out the cricks. It was eight am. He was punctual, as always. He heard Dinah come down the stairs and headed to the kitchen to give her some privacy. He pulled two mugs out of the cabinet and started making coffee, sticking two slices of toast in the toaster for Dinah.

'Hi Eric,' he heard her trill into the phone. She sounded fake

- he could hear the sadness in her voice even though her bravado. Why didn't Eric?

‘Yes, I'm fine. Tonight, I er...I'm not sure to be honest. I've been pulling a few doubles lately. I know. Nothing's wrong, don't worry. I'm fine. Just busy at work, I keep telling you. Listen, I have to get to work. I just got my car back on the road, but payday's next week.’

He could hear the muffled whine of Eric. He wouldn't be put off forever. To be fair, Gill was surprised he hadn't come to the door yet. If it had been him, he would have noticed the difference in her voice, been on her doorstep. He heard her end the call as he was buttering the toast. She came into the kitchen in her nurse's uniform, giving him a weak smile.

‘Is that for me? You don't have to make me breakfast you know.’ He pushed the plate across the island to her, and she sat down on one of the stools. Gill put some bread in for himself and passed her coffee over. She took it and sipped, a look of relief on her face. ‘Oh God I needed this. Thanks, is there any -’

Gill pushed across the jar of marmalade. Dinah looked at him and took the jar. ‘Thanks. Are you going to work today? I need to go back. I can't get any more time off, and the mortgage is due as well, so I need to make some hours up.’

‘I wasn't going to, but if you are then I will. Rory's pretty busy, I think. What about tonight?’

Dinah spread the marmalade thickly on her toast. Gill passed his plate across and she did the same to his without being asked. They were getting used to each other, living in such close proximity.

‘I can't keep you sleeping here, I know that sofa is awful. I need to get on with things really. Eric's getting moody, I need to see him and explain. Or lie altogether, like I have been doing. I'm not sure.'

'I don't mind staying, I keep telling you, I can cope with a few nights on the couch. Or I can buy an air bed. It's no bother.' He wanted to ask her about Eric, but he stopped himself. Truth was, he was happy to be there.

Dinah shook her head. 'I am so grateful Gill, really I am but you have your own life to live. You have your business with Rory, and I'm sure your family are missing you too.'

Gill snorted. 'My mother is, she wants me to meet some perfect girl from the synagogue. Apparently, she's just right for me, I think she already has us married off in her head.'

Dinah finished off her toast. 'My aunt's just the same. She has some hotty in mind for me too. Apparently, he's quite the catch. Which is why, of course, he's single and being auctioned off with the other single losers by his relatives.' She thought about her words and laughed. 'Sorry, that's us too, isn't it?'

'Hey, I'm just glad you're Jewish. It's nice to have someone who understands.' Eric wasn't Jewish. Did that mean he wasn't really anything serious?

'Yes, it really is,' she nodded, smiling at him.

Gill took the stool next to the door, taking a large gulp of his coffee. He pushed the toast plate between them, and she took another slice. She looked a little better today, like she had some colour back. She still needed to eat though.

'Listen, why don't you come to mine tonight? Get a change of scene? I have a spare room, you could stay over. I make a mean oven pizza and chips.'

Dinah bit her lip. 'I couldn't do that, I'll be fine honestly.' She didn't look convinced.

Gill reached for her hand. 'Dinah, it's no problem, I don't want you to be alone, and I could do with a night in my own bed. It'll do you good to get a change of scene.'

She nodded. 'Thanks, it would be nice actually. Shall I come straight after work? I could pack a bag now.'

Gill nodded, kissing her on the forehead as he went to grab his clothes. They both froze momentarily, both in shock at the sudden easy contact, but they hide it well.

'Yes, I'll lock up here. I have the spare key. See you tonight, okay?' He was just leaving the room when he felt her arms around him. She squeezed him tight to her.

'Thanks Gill. You should meet that girl, she would love you, I know it.'

He placed his hands over her arms and pulled her tighter into his back. He didn't trust himself to speak. 'Maybe. See you tonight, okay?'

CHAPTER FOURTEEN

Saturday morning

Early morning. Six am and Rory was at the gym. He was saying these words to himself in his head over and over again as he jogged on the treadmill. It's Saturday morning. Six am. I am at the gym. It's Saturday morning. Six am. I am at the gym. Lee was on the treadmill next to him, chatting away to Tim about the rugby results the day before. When he had agreed to go to the gym at the school gates, he didn't imagine for one minute that Lee would hold him to it, but when he called yesterday, it seemed a foregone conclusion. After the weekend he had endured so far, he figured that sweating out his frustrations might not be the worst thing after all. So here he was. At the gym, with two of the school dads - both of who worked physical jobs and took the gym as a daily ritual, like having a shower. Rory did run with Gill, but that was always kind of a relaxed time for them both, the equivalent of shopping for women. They ran a few miles, stopped for coffee, chatted about work. He really needed to check in with Gill, see what was happening. He had emailed and texted him about some client stuff, so things must have improved. He had sounded brighter, but then again, a text message could be interpreted a hundred different ways. He would know as soon as he set eyes on him how he was really feeling.

'So,' Lee said, turning to him and flicking a few sweat droplets his way, 'are you dating Annabel's mum?'

Rory shook his head. 'Nah, we're just friends. I'm Annabel's godfather.'

Tim looked at Lee, and back at Rory. They both looked him up and down. He was wearing tight lycra sports shorts, a running top and a white headband. All new of course, straight from the sports shop the day before, along with a pair of running trainers with an eye-watering price tag. The man in the shop had been very helpful of course, helping him to kit himself out for the gym. Towels, bag, water bottles. Rory had taken his suggestions and bought the lot, although he hadn't called to the pharmacy to buy Vaseline as he had been advised. In all honesty, he would rather live with chafed nipples than rub cream on them.

'Ah,' Tim said suddenly, as though something from his outfit had solved the puzzle in his head. 'I get it, sorry man. I didn't realise.' Lee looked at him and Tim nudged him. 'Rory, he's - you know, man.' Lee looked bewildered but then jolted in recognition. He slapped his own chest as though scolding himself. Rory was intent on trying to stay on the treadmill.

'What? I'm what?'

Tim pressed the stop button on his treadmill, slowing his steps. 'Hey listen, I have a ton of guys I could set you up with. Some really nice guys, too. If you're looking, obviously. No pressure.'

Rory slammed his hand down on the button and stepped off. 'Guys, I'm not gay. What made you think I was gay?'

Lee jumped off and the three men stood panting, reaching for their towels and bottles of water. 'It's ok Ror, it's no big deal. Honestly.' The two men nodded heads in unison.

'Guys, I'm not gay. I'm dating. A woman. A hot woman actually. Sarah and I have been friends since school, that's all. She's my best friend, has been since we were kids. I'm Annabel's godfather.' He didn't know why he felt the need to repeat that.

The two men glanced at each other. 'So, why the clothes then?' Lee asked. Rory felt a sudden urge to rip the sales assistant's head off.

'What? Is it bad?'

Tim sniggered, but managed to pass it off as a cough. 'No dude, you might want to rethink the headband though. So, if you're not dating Sarah, does that mean she's single?' He wiped off his glistening muscles with his towel. 'Because I've seen her at school and she's pretty nice. Any chance I could get her number? Me and my ex are on good terms, there's no drama there. I would really like to take her out.' He pulled a business card from his personal training business out of his shorts pocket and held it out to Rory. 'Would you give her my card?'

Rory looked at the card and his heart flopped into his boots. Another man wanting to take Sarah out. Thinking about Greg made his blood boil. The dude was a douchebag, and he had no intention of letting him near Sarah again, but Tim? He was a pretty nice guy. Lee was too, a devoted family man, and the two had known each other for years. He knew that they were both great dads from what he had seen at parties, play dates, the school yard. He had a good job, was financially independent. He had a nice car. He was what any single mum would deem to be 'good on paper'. Rory got on with him too, which was a bonus, and he knew Bunny would like him. So, what was stopping him from taking the card? He could feel himself staring at it as though he could make it spontaneously combust. Tim moved his hand closer. 'Ror, will you give it to her then?'

Rory took it, plastering a fake grin on his face. 'Of course, mate. I'm seeing her for lunch.' If she shows. 'I'll talk to her then.'

'Weights before we go?' Lee ventured. Rory went with them, but inside his head he could hear himself screaming.

Saturday morning, and Sarah woke up at eight o'clock with a huge smile on her face. She'd slept like a log, and for once she hadn't been woken up by her phone ringing or the panicked urge to check for messages. She hadn't heard from Greg since the night in the club, and it felt great. Annabel was happier, the extra pay for the admin work at the club meant she didn't miss his paltry allowance, and her mother had relaxed for the first time in months. So relaxed in fact, that she was singing downstairs. Sarah strained to listen. She could hear music, and the sound of Annabel laughing.

She threw on her robe and slippers and headed downstairs. In the hallway, she stopped in shock. The record player lid was open for the first time in years. There was a record playing on the turntable. Etta James, At Last, to be exact. One of Mum's favourites. She went over and touched the side of the player, thinking of the times she had listened to these records as a child. She felt like Dad was there, for a moment, and her heart squeezed at the memory. Just hearing the sound of this song lifted the mood of the house. It was as though it had woken up. She walked into the kitchen and could have cried at the sight. Her mother was dancing, swaying to the music with Annabel in her arms. They were both swaying and singing to the music, just like she had done with her as a child, while her father looked on. Sarah leant against the doorframe, hanging back so they wouldn't see her. Bunny looked beautiful. She was all dressed up, hair done and singing her heart out.

Bunny had such a beautiful voice, but she hadn't sung in years, aside from the lullabies she sang to Annabel every night. The last bars of the song rang out and her mother and daughter sang them out loud, twirling each other around. Sarah stepped forward when the music stopped. Bunny spied her in the doorway. They didn't say a word to each other. They didn't need to, they knew that they were both feeling the same emotions. Sarah went to them both, wrapping her arms around the pair in a group hug.

'Morning, Mummy!' Annabel said, red cheeked with happiness. 'Nana got out the records!'

'I know, baby.'

Bunny smiled. 'Fantastic isn't it?'

Sarah looked at her mother and dropped a kiss onto her cheek. 'It sure is. I think you should have started pottery class years ago. What shall we play next?'

An hour later, Rory was standing outside Sarah's door, ringing the bell for the twentieth time. It sounded like next door was playing Motown classics - he could hear Gloria Gaynor. He buzzed again. Her car was outside, as was Bunny's, so they must be in. He got his phone out and rang her number again. No answer. She knew he was coming at nine to pick them up. He knocked again and heard a shriek from inside. His blood went cold. Greg! Stuffing his phone into his jacket pocket, he tried the door. It opened. He crept into the hall, grabbed an umbrella from the stand in the corner, and ran to the noise. The music's playing in here, his brain registered belatedly as he threw himself through the doors, thrusting the umbrella out in front of him.

'Leave them alone, dirtbag!' He shouted, lowering himself

into a ninja stance. He was greeted by three high pitched screams, and a thump on the arm. 'Ow!'

Something hit Rory square on the foot, and since he was wearing a trendy canvas shoe, slammed straight into his toes. 'Arrgghh!' He shouted, bending double with the pain. 'You'll pay for that, you scoundrel!'

Three sets of laughing voices suddenly erupted and Rory looked up from his foot. Bunny, Sarah and Annabel were all in hysterics, Bunny slapping the worktop and holding her stomach, Sarah with Annabel wrapped around her. It was then he registered that the object at his feet was one of Bunny's rolling pins, and the weapon he had chosen was a child's umbrella with a T-Rex emblazoned on it. It had unfurled, and he now looked like he was about to perform a samurai style version of Singing in the Rain.

'You're okay?' He said, looking around whilst trying to shut the brolly. 'I thought, I heard...why is the music on?'

The women recovered, and Sarah came across to him. 'We were dancing. Mum had her old records on. I didn't hear you knock, sorry!' Bunny was unbuttoning his cuff, lifting his shirt sleeve up to inspect his arm. He had a red mark, presumably from where Bunny had thrown the rolling pin at him.

'Oooh love, that's going to leave a mark! I'm sorry pet, you just startled me, and I grabbed for the first thing I could see.' She took the brolly from him, folding it up in one smooth movement. 'I see you did the same.' She looked at him, and Rory could see she was resisting the urge to laugh. Gloria was still singing out loud, and Sarah turned it down.

'Annabel, go get your backpack sweetie. Uncle Rory has a

surprise for you.'

'Uncle Rory did have a surprise,' he said sheepishly, after Annabel had thrown him a pitying look and run upstairs with Bunny in tow. 'But he now has crushed toes and a very deflated ego.'

'Aww, and you sounded like an old black and white film, too! Scoundrel?' Rory blushed, and Sarah grabbed him for an unexpected hug. 'I'm only kidding, I know why you came in. You were rescuing us, weren't you?'

He nodded, resting his chin on the top of her head and wrapping his arms around her. He could feel his heart beating fast in his chest. 'I was, yes. I thought Greg might have...'

'Nah, he hasn't been in touch. I think he's holed up with some woman somewhere. Poor cow.'

'As long as he isn't causing trouble here, I don't care where he is.' He felt Sarah squeeze him tighter and he kissed the top of her head. 'So, we all ready for a day out? I thought we could eat out too, there's a nice country pub not far away from where we're going. My treat?' Sarah looked at him and opened her mouth to argue but Rory pushed his finger over her lips. 'Ssh, don't flippin' argue with me today. I'm technically your boss now, so you have to do what I say.' He waggled his eyebrows.

'Oh really,' she said. The movement of her lips against his finger felt like a kiss, and he looked at them, falling silent. They both stood still, not moving as they looked at each other close up. Their eyes roamed over the other's features.

'Ready!' Bunny announced, walking into the room with a dragon backpack in her hands. She pulled an apologetic face. 'Sorry! I'll come back.' Annabel was stood behind her, looking at the pair of them with a strange expression on her face. The pair of them stood apart from each other, Rory clearing his throat. Sarah busied herself with the content of her handbag. 'You ready honey? Go get your coat.' Annabel grabbed Bunny's hand, pulling her gently but urgently to the stairs. Bunny looked back at the pair.

'Sorry I interrupted,' she said in a sad voice. She turned and let Annabel drag her up the staircase.

'Sarah -'

'So, big date tonight, eh? The big fight?' Sarah was slinging her oversized handbag over her shoulder, slotting in bottled water and cereal bars for the journey.

'Er, yes. Tonight, ringside seats apparently. What about you, how's things going with Neil?'

'Nigel,' Sarah corrected, heading to the hall to slip her boots on. 'It's going okay, we're going out tomorrow night actually. Dinner and a movie.'

Rory nodded his head slowly. 'Good, good.'

Annabel half dragged her grandmother up the stairs, pushing her into her bedroom and shutting the door firmly.

'What on earth is the matter?' Bunny said, flustered from the mad dash up the stairs. She took a seat on the bed to steady herself. 'Rory didn't scare you, did he? We were only joking. He would never hurt you.'

Annabel was halfway under her bed, and Bunny looked at her little legs hanging out. 'Annabel darling, don't hide under there. Everything's fine. Don't be scared.'

Annabel reverse commando crawled out from under the bed,

a show box decorated with stickers in her hands. 'Hurt me? I know that he wouldn't hurt me, and I'm not scared. He was trying to protect me from Dad.'

Bunny's face crumpled with shock. 'Oh Anna -'

Annabel sat down on the floor, putting her back to the door. 'It's okay Nana, I'm not a baby. I know what happened. I heard you and Rory's dad when you thought I was asleep. Dad hurt Mummy's friend. He's not a nice person. That's why I have a plan, and I want you to help.' She opened up the box, peeking at the door. 'We have to be quick.' She pulled out a notebook from the box, and Bunny recognised it as the one she had been carrying around of late. Inside were lists, drawings, cut out pictures stuck on every page.

Annabel turned to a page and Bunny blinked. She had drawn a heart, with pink and red crayons, and inside she had stuck in some pictures. Bunny recognised them from one of her albums downstairs. It was of Sarah and Rory, at the graduation celebration Bunny had organised when they finished university. They were both draped over each other, Rory's arms around her, and they were laughing into the camera. She remembered that night, Doug had been working late as usual, and hadn't made it in time for the whole meal, but the three of them had had such a wonderful night. She thought of the pair of them at her kitchen table, tucking into tea when they were not much older than Annabel was now.

'It's a nice picture hun, but what do you want to do? Is it a present for your mum?'

'No!' Annabel said, her determined little face getting pinched with frustration. She jabbed her little digit at the picture. 'This is what I want. Mummy and Uncle Roar-Roar. Together. With us.'

Bunny went to speak but closed her mouth again. Something she had seen downstairs made her think that Annabel, her smart as a whip granddaughter, might just be on to something. 'What about your dad?' she asked, already knowing the answer.

Annabel shook her head. 'He doesn't make Mummy happy, Rory does.' She flipped more pages, showing more photos of them over the years. The last photo was taken at the hospital. The day she was born. 'See?' Mummy smiles the most when Rory is there. The four of us.'

'I remember that day,' Bunny said fondly, motioning for her granddaughter to sit on her knee with the notebook. 'Your mother was amazing, and when you were born she was so happy. Your dad was on shift, so he missed you coming into the world, but I was right there with her.' She was stood next to the bed in the photograph, Sarah flushed, smiling with the tiny Annabel in her arms. She pointed to Rory, who was sitting half on the bed, looking at the camera, one hand around Sarah as though he was the doting new dad. He had been there for the whole thing, never wavering, never leaving her side, keeping Greg updated by text, even though he didn't or couldn't reply. It was one of the best days of Bunny's life. When she thought back, Rory was in most of those memories after Charlie had passed. 'Rory was so proud of your mother that day.'

They heard Sarah calling from them downstairs, and Rory called, 'Come on Belle, adventure and chocolate await!'

She hugged her granddaughter tight, giving her a big kiss. 'I'm in. I think I can ask someone else to help too.'

Annabel beamed and threw her arms around her nana. 'Operation Notebook is a go!'

CHAPTER FIFTEEN

Rory pulled his car into the zoo car park and they all looked out of the windows at the huge expanse of fields covered with different enclosures, pens and huts.

'So, they look after them here? They're not mistreated?' Annabel's huge eyes looked at him, clouded with concern.

Sarah smiled at him. 'Come on then, Ror, tell her.'

He got out of the car and opening her door, he waited for her to jump out. She reached for his hand and squealed when he threw her over his shoulders. 'I promise you, I looked into it. They work as conservationists, these animals are all saved from circuses, and other attractions. They work to save them here hun, and they run breeding programs too. Plus, they work on their carbon footprint in order to help combat global warming.' He nudged Sarah with his elbow as they walked up to the main gates, bags in hand. 'That good enough, eh Miss Jennings?'

'Not bad, Mr Gallant. Not bad at all. What do you think Annabel?'

Annabel leaned down and dropped a kiss on Rory's cheek. 'It's the best, I can't wait!'

Sarah hugged him, and they all walked into the zoo together.

Three hours later, and Rory thanked his lucky stars that he had worn comfy shoes. They had walked every inch of the park, Annabel enraptured with the animals, most of which she had renamed. They had taken a picnic bench near the park and were steadily tucking into the huge picnic Bunny had prepared for them while Annabel played on the play equipment.

'Look at her,' Sarah said, before tucking into a cheese and pickle sandwich. 'She never just plays like this, on playground equipment. She's normally too busy disinfecting the slide rails or trying to catalogue the flowers. She loves it here.'

Rory nodded, laughing. 'She gave that zoo keeper a run for her money, didn't she? I swear, when she went to Google something on her phone and found that Annabel was right, that was hilarious!'

'I know, right? I'm pretty sure she won't be allowed back here.'

Rory passed her a napkin and took a ham sandwich from the pile. 'This is nice.'

'I know, I'm really glad we did it. How about that woman, who thought Annabel was your daughter?' Sarah looked at him, and he looked back at her.

'She was sweet,' he replied. 'Nice lady.'

'Why didn't you correct her?' Sarah asked, looking at Annabel who was careering down the slide, laughing.

'I'm sorry, I didn't mean to upset you.'

Sarah was already shaking her head. 'No, you didn't upset me. I just wondered, why you didn't? Annabel didn't say anything either.'

Rory took a swig of his bottle of water, debating the answer himself. 'In all honesty, it's not the first time it's happened. I guess we look alike, so when people compliment me on her, or call me her dad, I just don't correct them. Annabel never does, so I just let it slide. I mean, why explain your business to strangers?'

Sarah nodded. 'Doesn't it cramp your style though, having a daughter?'

Rory laughed. 'Don't be daft. I love Annabel, I don't care what people think. She'll always be in my life.'

'What about Sasha though? Will she understand? You hanging out with some woman's daughter?'

Rory scowled. 'Why is this a thing? Are you trying to tell me something?'

She reached for his hand and took it in hers. 'No, sorry, of course not. I just...things are changing. For both of us. Greg is…well, Greg. You're with Sasha, and I'm dating. It's just a lot of adjustment for Annabel, and I just wondered where you were at.'

He looked at Annabel, who turned and waved at them both. She looked at them holding hands and grinned.

'Whoops,' Sarah said, pulling back. Rory reached for her hand again.

'Sarah, don't be daft. I've seen you give birth, us holding hands is nothing to shock people over.'

'Oooh, don't remind me,' she groaned. 'I did tell you to stay at the head end. That stuff can't be unseen.'

Rory chuckled. 'When you kicked that nurse in the head, that was hilarious.'

Sarah sniggered. 'I was high on gas and air, she was annoying me.' They both laughed together, and the awkwardness between them dissipated.

'Do you ever wonder what things would have been like, if we had met later in life?'

Rory frowned. 'It would have been awful, I don't like that idea. I don't remember us not being in each other's lives.' Sarah didn't answer. 'What's this about Sar?'

Sarah looked at him and willed herself to tell him how confused she felt. Since that moment in Doug's office, when they almost kissed, things had been confusing to her. Was it just because he was dating now, changing his appearance for another woman? Was that what this was, jealousy? A fear of being left behind?

They had been at the monkey enclosure, and a handler had just placed one of their tame monkeys on their laps, so that Annabel and Sarah could get a photo with him. Rory was just taking the photo when an elderly couple came up behind them. She had tapped him on the shoulder.

'You have a beautiful family,' she said innocently, smiling at him. He'd looked back at Sarah, her daughter in her arms, and felt a surge of love.

'Thanks,' he replied, grinning back. 'I know I'm very lucky.' It seemed like the most natural thing in the world to him. She was his family, they both were.

'That's what this is about? The lady when we were taking the photo?'

'Yes, and no. I just mean, things could have been different, I think, and I just wondered...' Rory looked at her blankly, and she sighed. 'Rory, I'm just talking daft. Don't worry about it.'

He nodded slowly, itching to press her on what she was trying to say. He remembered Tim's card then from this morning, and he put his hand into his pocket to give it to her. His hand closed around it, but he didn't pull it out. He looked at their entwined fingers and his gut clenched. He pushed it deeper into his pocket instead and covered her hand between his. 'When we're done eating, let's go via the candy floss stand. We still have the seals to see.'

Sarah nodded, giving his hand a squeeze.

From the climbing frame, Annabel watched her mum and Rory, talking hand in hand. She saw Rory brush a stray strand of windswept hair from her face as they laughed with each other, and she shook her head. Human adults, they had to be the dumbest species when it came to finding a mate.

CHAPTER SIXTEEN

Saturday night

Leon drew back his right hook and smashed it into the side of his opponent's head, while the crowd bayed all around him. The arena was packed, the spotlights showing the sweat and steam coming off the two opponents as they danced around each other. The spectators all around them were off their seats, screaming at the boxers, shouting out curses, tactics, cheering their chosen side on. Leon Mendez was impressive. He was massive anyway, Rory had seen that for himself on the posters, and from in the club that night, but in the ring, wow. The man looked like he had been carved from pure muscle, and he was using every inch of it against his opponent. In the moment he looked as though he was a machine, not a man. The reaction from the crowd as he moved around the ring with his sparring partner was amazing. People changed when they watched a sport like this. It wasn't like golf, with civilised clapping in posh slacks. Or tennis, where people moved their necks like oscillating fans whilst eating strawberries and cream and drinking Pimms. This, right here, was another world and Rory was sat right in the thick of it. He might not be enamoured by it, but he could see the attraction it held for others.

Sasha was dressed for the occasion. She was glowing in a tight cream dress, faux fur coat wrapped around her against the chill of the arena. She was standing next to him, screaming at Mendez, face flushed with excitement. Rory was standing next to her, but he wasn't looking at the match. He was looking at her. She was so beautiful, her red hair even more vibrant against the cream of her outfit. Several men had looked at her when they walked in. She was obviously used to the attention, because she never acknowledged the stares or drools that came her way. She turned to him, stroking him on the arm.

'You having fun? Amazing, isn't he?' She was shouting over the crowd now, and he smiled at her.

'He is, it's pretty brutal though, right?' She laughed then, squeezing his arm close.

'I know, it's fantastic!' She pulled him in close, and grabbing the back of his head, she put her lips to his. He was startled, but soon kissed her back. He could taste her lipstick, and the vodka she had been sipping from. She was taking the lead in the kiss, and he let her. She kissed him deeper, dipping her tongue into his mouth a little before turning into him and putting her hands on his chest under his jacket. She wrapped her arms around him, and he pulled her in further. Her coat tickled his nose as he kissed her, but he ignored it. He was here in the moment, with the girl of his dreams, and she was kissing him! It was exactly what he wanted, albeit not in these circumstances.

A flash of Sarah, laughing at the zoo with him earlier that day, her face lit up in the sunlight, popped into his head. He pushed it away, tried to pull himself back into the moment. He felt as though all eyes were on him, everyone cheering him on. The nice guy finally got the girl. The crowd erupted, and Sasha broke off the kiss to look at the fight.

'He won!' She said, clapping excitedly. 'He won, Rory!' She kissed him again and wrapped her arm around his back. He tucked her into him, feeling elated and more than a little glad that the fight was over. Mendez's opponent was on the floor, and the crowd were cheering and chanting 'Mendez! Mendez!' Sasha turned to Rory. ‘Come on darling, we have a big party to go to.’ She took him by the hand and led him through the crowds to the security team that were congregated by the doors leading to the changing rooms.

‘Guys, what a night eh? We alright to wait in the changing rooms for him?’ The security guys looked from her to Rory. She lifted their hands that were still clasped together. ‘He's with me tonight.’

They were nodded through and led to a large changing area off the left hand side of the long corridor. Inside were showers in the back, lockers, and equipment laid out. On the other side was a green room set up, comfy chairs and sofas complete with a buffet table along the back wall with covered trays, lines of drinks bottles and champagne on ice.

‘Wow, he was optimistic. Did he expect to win?’ From working in the club, he knew there was some serious money here, in the alcohol alone.

Sasha lifted one of the trays and seemingly satisfied, replaced the cover. ‘I organised this, from the firm. Win or lose, Leon will make a bundle tonight, for the firm and for us, on ticket sales alone. Plus, we have merchandise, advertising and sponsorship. You've seen the big matches they have on Sky, there's a lot of money in boxing. Win or lose, it's another step on his career path. Mendez is going to be massive.’

Rory, being a money man, could appreciate what she was saying, what he knew it meant for her job, but boxing still wasn't for him. He wondered how many events of these she had planned, how many she might want him to attend.

'So, you're branching into people, rather than products? So you get more tiers of consumer spending to work with, right?'

Sasha poured them both a glass of champagne. 'You know your stuff, Rory. I'm impressed. And yet I still don't know what you do. I know you have connections to the club, but that's all. You know the business though, right?' She sashayed over, passing him a flute of bubbles. 'So, we've had two dates. I know your name, and that you're a good kisser. I pride myself on knowing all about people, but you…you're pretty quiet. Something of an enigma. There's nothing on social media either, so you don't have any accounts. What do you do, Mr Gallant? Doug was pretty tight lipped, and I'm not sure your PA likes me.'

She walked her fingers up his chest and Rory shivered from her touch. 'Aww,' she said, a sly grin on her face. 'Do I make you nervous, Rory?'

Rory wanted to tell her yes, that he had looked at her in the club for weeks and always wanted to speak to her but couldn't. She called him Ryan then though, and she obviously didn't still remember him. Obviously, the contact lenses worked. Rory had always thought it ridiculous that Lois Lane never recognised Superman as Clark Kent without his glasses, but here they were.

'I'm in finance, yes. You rumbled my secret. I do have an interest in the club, in fact I'm going to be managing it more in the future.'

'Oh really, taking more of a hands on approach?' She moved her fingers further up, running her long nails along the side of his neck, the line of his chin. He could feel himself reacting to her touch, and he tried his best to project a neutral expression onto his face. He took a sip of champagne, giving himself a minute to collect himself. 'Listen, how about tonight, we -'

She was interrupted by increasingly loud voices coming from outside, and the door burst open, Leon striding in followed by half a dozen guards and his entourage. They were all chattering away to each other. Rory took a slight step back, aware that it might look a little unprofessional, but Sasha didn't move. Leon spotted her and banged his gloves together.

'What about that then, Sash? We did it, boo!'

He came forward, scooping her up in his big sweaty arms as his colleagues all set to work on the food and drinks. A sound system Rory hadn't noticed before was fired up and hip-hop tunes started blasting out. Sasha squealed in his arms.

'I told you baby! Well done! Wembley Arena here we come!' He lifted her higher and she giggled, grasping his face in between her hands. Rory was just thinking how nice it was that Sasha was such good friends with her clients, when she lowered her head and dropped a smacker on the boxer's lips. The onlookers all whooped and cheered, and a man stood at the side of Rory nudged him.

'That girl there, is pure class. She will do anything for Leon, man. Anything. Best thing he ever did was sign with her.'

Rory looked at the man who was currently twirling Sasha in the air whilst sucking her face off. 'Yeah, I can see that.'

No, boxing definitely wasn't his cup of tea. And when he thought of pure class, he didn't picture Sasha. Sarah, she was pure class. She would never behave like this. He suddenly wished she was here, hating the boxing as much as he did and poking fun at the antics of the baying crowd.

Rory came out of the arena doors and pulled his jacket around him a bit tighter. It was quite chilly, the early summer nights still a little cool. He headed to the car park, looking for his Volvo. He got his keys out of his pocket and realised with a start that he was looking for a car he didn't even own anymore. He looked at the Audi key fob on his key chain. Well, he looked the part, and he still hadn't got the girl. What the hell was going on?

'Rory, wait up!' Sasha called from behind him. She half ran after him, her heels clattering on the tarmac. 'Where did you get to? Micky said you left!'

He turned around, waiting for her to apologise. She looked at him in confusion. 'I didn't realise you couldn't stay, you going to the club? You should have said, I think we'll be headed there later, if you have space in the VIP area. The venue here is a bit too generic for my liking.' She came closer, moving in to kiss him. Rory pulled back.

'I don't think so.'

'What?' She put her hands on his chest, and he caught them in his, pulling them away. 'Rory, what's the matter?' She looked at him as if the answer was on his face. Realisation dawned, and she started to laugh. 'Awww, come on - Leon? It was only a kiss, I'm not with the guy.'

Rory put her hands down by her sides and released them. 'Sorry, but on dates, I'm not used to watching my date kiss someone else. It kinda kills the mood a bit. I don't share.' Wow, that was alpha male. Well done, Ror. Claim that dignity back with the plan.

'So, you were leaving?' She held her hands out in question. 'Over a friendly kiss? I'm in PR, Leon is a client, a friend, what's the big deal? We've been on two dates Rory, we're not married.'

Rory said nothing, just turned to walk to his car. 'I can give you a lift home if you like.' He had picked her up from the office, and the gentleman in him couldn't leave her without making sure she got home safe.

'Rory, I'm sorry - I didn't realise it would offend you. I wasn't even sure you liked me that much, in all honesty. You keep your cards pretty close, and I don't know much about you. Can we start again?'

He stopped and turned around to face her. 'What about Leon?'

Sasha shrugged, tossing her hair over her shoulder. 'Leon is a client, there's nothing in it. I won't kiss him again, if that's the issue.' Rory raised his eyebrows at her words.

'No, it wasn't the best move. Don't let it happen again.'

She moved towards him, and he stood still, holding her gaze with what he hoped was a steely one of his own. 'Ok, no more kissing other people. Now I know. Can we move on now? I have to get back to Leon, but shall we see you at the club, later?' She raised a perfectly sculpted brow in question.

'I'll behave, I promise.'

'Hey!' Sarah said, as Rory came out of the wash room. 'What are you doing here?'

'Er, I work here?' The bar was thriving, and Sarah had three staff on her bar. People were flush from pay day and looking to blow off some steam from the week at work.

'I know that numb nuts, I mean what are you doing here, behind the bar, when you should be watching two men punch the living snot out of each other for money?' Sarah shared his dislike of boxing. He grabbed a glass and put it under the optic.

'Oh, and drinking too. I hope you are going to pay for that, our accountant is a real hardass.'

Rory pulled a double whisky and slugged it back in one. His throat burned but it soothed his nerves. He felt decidedly weird about the night's events. Sasha was not turning out how he expected her to be, and his own behaviour in response had thrown him for a loop. Normally, he would have just taken that behaviour, but following the plan had made him brave. Mean, and angry, but brave. He felt glad that he'd called Sasha out on her behaviour. It was wrong, and she needed to understand that he wasn't going to accept it.

'Hardi-har-har. Annabel get to sleep on time? I didn't think she could eat that much candy floss.'

Sarah laughed, taking his glass from him and putting it with the dirty ones before he could pour another. 'She did actually, she crashed before I left. I really thought she was going to throw up in your car on the way home. I couldn't get that giraffe out of her hands though, she went to sleep with it in her arms. You're mad you know, spoiling her like that.'

Rory shrugged. 'She's my godchild, it's my job. Sasha's coming later, she's bringing some of the boxing lot with her. I came earlier to set up the VIP area. Should be a good night for the club.'

'And the date?' Sarah took an empty optic down, putting the bottle into the bottle bank and washing the optic out before replacing it with a fresh bottle. 'How did it go with Sasha?' She mimed tossing her hair dramatically. He thought of her going out with Nigel.

'It went really well,' Rory lied. 'We're going to continue it later.' Seeing her shocked expression, he jolted at his own choice of words. 'Here! Here I mean, in the club, that's all. Nothing like that yet.' Though she did suck face with a mountain of muscle right in front of me and a room full of people. Does that count? 'We did kiss, actually.' Sarah was serving a regular, and she kept working.

'Did you hear me?' he checked. She served the next customer and started wiping down the bar. 'Sar?'

'I heard you. So how was it?'

Rory noticed a man pointing them out to two other men. The three of them started coming over. 'It was fine, do you know them?' He jerked his head in their direction and moved closer to her. He had a bad feeling about the way they were looking at Sarah. 'Sar, go to the wash room. I can get someone to serve them.'

Sarah looked across. 'What the hell is he doing here?' She said, under her breath. Rory reached for her and was about to pick her up and carry her through the wash room doors when she smiled at one of the men.

'Hi!' She said sweetly, pulling her arm gently out of Rory's grasp, shooting him an odd look before pulling away. 'What are you doing here?'

The man looked at his friends and back at Sarah sheepishly. 'I'm on a night out. We thought we'd come for a drink.' He looked to Rory, who looked poised to murder him. 'Is that okay, or should we go?'

'No, no, it's lovely. Listen, this is Rory, my er...boss. Can I take my break now?' Rory was still staring at the man, an odd look on his face.

'Boss,' she said pointedly. 'Can I take my break now, with Nigel?'

Rory snapped back into the conversation. Nigel. Her date. Right. 'Er..yes! Yes, of course. Go on, take your break. No problem.'

Sarah nodded and shuffled off to the wash room. Nigel looked nice, he'd certainly made the effort. He looked at Rory.

'Hi, Rory is it? Thanks for letting her take her break. I'm just out with some friends and wanted to see her. I'm planning to take her out for lunch tomorrow.'

'No problem,' he said, remembering that Sarah said she was planning to take the day off tomorrow. 'Annabel going with you?'

Nigel looked around at the staff. Frankie was stood near by, and he gave her a cursory nod. 'Er no, no friends, just the two of us I think.' He turned to Frankie with an apologetic look on his face. 'Don't mind, do you?'

Frankie heard him and flashed a look at Rory. Rory opened up his mouth to correct him, but Frankie stepped in first.

'I have plans anyway hun, don't worry. I have a hot date with a duvet and a good book.' She winked at Nigel, and he looked relieved.

'What are you guys talking about?' Sarah said, as he came and stood next to Nigel. His two friends were now eyeing up a couple of girls who were dancing on the large lit up dance floor and paying no notice to what was going on. Nigel put his arm around Sarah, and she moved into him awkwardly, looking anywhere but at Rory.

'I was just talking to Annabel about taking you out for lunch tomorrow, just us.'

Sarah froze momentarily, and Frankie smiled at her. 'Hope you have a good lunch. I'm going to be laid in bed reading my new romance book. First day off in months, I can't wait.'

Rory couldn't hear anymore, he left the bar and stood in the wash room. Why the hell did he think Annabel was Frankie? It was obvious that he didn't know about Annabel. Why wouldn't she tell him? It made him so angry, but he didn't want to show her up more than he already had. It was a good job he hadn't mentioned the zoo trip they had just been on that day. She seemed to like him though. Did he not like kids? Was it because of Greg? If she hadn't told him about her daughter, Rory was betting the subject of the deranged baby daddy hadn't come up either. Maybe that was the reason, but still. What kind of future could they have if they didn't tell each other the important details of their lives? He seemed like a decent guy, he wouldn't be put off by a child, surely? Rory was stomping through the club now, ignoring the vibration of the mobile phone in his pocket. It was probably his dad to check on the club, or a text from Sarah chewing him out. She probably wouldn't be best pleased that he had let slip, but how the hell was he to know? If Annabel was his, he would shout it from the rooftops, not keep her hidden away. He was always proud to be out with her, and Sarah. Was what why he was so mad? He headed through the revellers to the offices, heaving a sigh of relief when the doors slammed shut, cutting off the noise of the club. His phone rang again as he headed to his office, and he slammed it into his desk drawer without looking at it.

The fantastic Saturday night he had been hoping for hadn't been remotely what he was expecting. He poured himself a large whisky, pulling some ice chips from the tub in the mini freezer. His dad had things set up well here. He had snacks in the fridge, soft drinks, mixers. Enough whiskey to sterilize a zebra. It was so quiet, just what he needed to collect his thoughts. He sat down on the leather sofa, kicking off his shoes and letting his feet breathe. The damn trendy shoes were pinching him. They said fashion before comfort, well he was definitely feeling that tonight. He loosened his tie and laid it on the sofa back, taking a big draw of his drink. A flash of Sasha in Leon's arms, kissing him, came into his thoughts and he winced at the memory. He had never expected anything like that to happen, and now, somehow, he had been talked into playing host for Sasha and her tonsil hockey partner in crime. Meanwhile Sarah was on some mini date with Neil/Nigel...whatever. How the hell had all of this happened?

His phone rang again in his drawer, and he put his head back on the leather. Bugger off. It rang off, and the phone on the desk rang instead. Groaning, he dragged himself over and picked it up.

'Rory,' he said, sounding defeated in his own ears.

'Rory,' Winston drawled. 'You have incoming. Look at the monitor.'

Rory looked at the television monitor. On the CCTV, he could see Sasha, Leon and the people from the entourage all getting stamped into reception. 'Okay Winston, that's fine - just stamp them all in. Get security to check them and take them all to the main VIP area. Everything's ready.'

'That's fine boss, but we have an extra guest.'

Rory looked again at the screen, wondering what Winston was talking about, till he saw who was talking to Leon. They seemed to be laughing together, having a good time. Did they know each other?

'Winston, is Leon asking for him to come in?'

Winston looked straight at the camera. 'Yep, saw him waiting outside. Apparently, they go way back. You want me to door stop him?'

Rory looked again at the screen, at Greg's smug, laughing little face. He was posing for a photographer outside, arm in arm with Leon. 'No, we can't afford the bad press. Tell Nathan to send an extra body to the VIP area, watch him like a hawk. Sarah's on a break in the club, so keep eyes on. I'm on my way.'

Draining his glass, he looked at the monitor. Sasha was oblivious to any tension, as always, but Rory could see that Winston and the other door staff weren't best pleased to be having Greg in the foyer. Greg, however, was clearly loving every minute. He would know Leon, of course. The smug twat probably went boxing with him or something. It was going to be a long night. They started to move towards the main doors, and Rory grabbed his stuff and ran out of the door. He jogged down the corridor, hurriedly putting on his tie, shoving his feet back into his shoes. He slipped out of the doors and could just see Nathan and Ian bringing the party towards the VIP area. He stayed out of their eye line, heading for the main bar. Sarah wasn't behind it. Shit. He half ran up to it, beckoning to Frankie.

'Where's Sarah, did you see where she went?' Frankie shook her head.

'No, sorry. What's up?'

'Greg's here. I can't bar him tonight, long story.'

Frankie rolled her eyes. 'Awesome. Go find her Ror, before he sees her with Nigel.'

Rory headed to the other side of the bar, away from the VIP area where there were some booths in the quieter area. He scanned the area and noticed the two lads that were stood with Nigel. They were both knocking out awkward looking shapes next to a couple of very bemused women, but Nigel and Sarah were missing. He turned to scan each booth and spotted her. They had their heads together, and for a stomach lurching second, he thought that they were kissing, but then Sarah gestured with her hand and he could see that they were just talking, heads close together to hear each other over the music. He walked over, and she spotted him over Nigel's shoulder.

'Rory, what's wrong? I still have ten minutes left on my break.' Her tone was annoyed, and he could see that she was pissed at him for earlier. Nigel ignored him completely, taking Sarah's hand in his.

'I know, I'm sorry - it's just…' He needed to get her away, back behind the bar where he could keep Greg away from her, hopefully Nigel too. But how? He took a deep breath. She was mad at him anyway, so to hell with it.

'I'm sorry Sarah, but we're very busy tonight, and you chatting with your boyfriend in the club isn't on. Breaks are for the break room, and we have a VIP party coming in.' He looked at Nigel coolly. 'If you could leave the premises please, we don't encourage relationships at work. You are a distraction to Sarah. Your friends are welcome to stay of course, and I will refund your entry fee for this evening.' He pointed his arm to the door, and Nigel looked at him in disbelief.

'Seriously?' he asked, looking from him to Sarah.

'Seriously. If you don't leave quietly now, I'll have to call security.'

Sarah was looking at him as if he had sprouted another head, but then she pulled Nigel to face her. 'It's okay Nigel, you go - I'll see you tomorrow for lunch, okay? I'll call you in the morning.'

Nigel looked back at Rory, as if he was hoping to develop laser vision in the next twenty seconds and blast a hole in his face.

'Fine,' he said, fighting the urge to be mad with the need to be a gentleman and a good guy in front of the girl he wanted to impress. 'Call me tomorrow.'

Sarah nodded and started to shimmy out of the booth, but Nigel pulled her back and taking her face in his arms, he kissed her. Sarah jumped, and Rory could see Nigel was making more of the kiss than she was. The whole thing was awkward to watch. You might as well just pee all over her, Nige. Sarah broke off the kiss, muttering a bye to Nigel and walking briskly back to the bar. Her arm brushed against Rory's, but she never acknowledged him, keeping her eyes firmly ahead of her. Nigel grinned at Rory, wiping the lipstick from his mouth and licking his lips.

'Well, that was nice. I can't wait for tomorrow.' He stood up, walking slowly over to Rory in a cocky saunter. 'You know, when Sarah and I go on another date, all alone.'

Rory felt his jaw clench tight, and his hands tighten into fists at his sides. 'Yes, well, good night.'

Nigel stopped an inch from Rory. 'Jealous, are we? You make all these rules, but you want to bang the staff, right?'

He jabbed his finger into Rory's chest. Rory could feel his heart hammer. This guy was another Greg, it was written all over his smug, supercilious face. The thought of him being with Sarah made Rory's blood sizzle in his veins.

'You touch me again, I'll snap that finger clean off. I know your type, and Sarah is too good for you. She'll see it before too long, I'll make sure of it. Now get the fuck out of my club.'

Nigel's friends came over, flanking him. 'What's up Nige? Where's Sarah?'

Nigel and Rory never took their eyes off each other. 'She's gone back to work. I'm going to a better club, you coming, or staying?' The two men glanced back at the women, who were now dry humping a couple of fresh blokes on the dance floor behind them.

'Yeah, let's go.' The three men headed to the main doors, Nigel slamming his shoulder into Rory's as a parting shot as he passed. Rory laughed, giving them a little wave when they looked back. He reached for his phone, realising it was still in his drawer. He headed to the foyer, following their movements as they swaggered like peacocks out of the doors. He pointed them out to Winston when he went into the booth.

'Those three don't get back in. Ever.' Winston nodded.

'No problem, boss.'

Sasha was chatting to Leon's manager when Rory eventually went past. He could see Sarah serving drinks behind the bar, but she didn't look his way when he tried to catch her eye. The look on her face said it all though. He headed to the offices, keeping close to the outer walls of the club and staying in the shadows to avoid the VIP area. He could see Sasha, she kept looking around her into the sea of faces. She was looking for him. He'd have to be quick. Calling at the smaller bar near the office doors, he instructed a bottle of the best champagne be sent over with the compliments of the club for his big win. It would keep her happy.

He headed straight for his office, checking the cameras were all looking okay as he reached for his phone. It was after eleven o'clock. He scrolled through his missed calls, seeing some from Sasha, the box office here (Winston) and his dad once. He hit send on his number. His dad answered after a few rings.

'Hi son,' he said. 'How's the club going?'

'Fine Dad, we have the boxer in, VIP. Listen, I know it's late, but could you possibly go over to Bunny's?'

His dad spluttered on the phone. 'Er, why would you want me to go there? I haven't seen Bunny since that night. I…er...'

Rory heard a shuffle on the phone line, something sounding like a large slap. 'Dad, I know that. It's just -'

'Greg. I get it, sorry. Is he at the club, or gone?'

Rory glanced at the monitors, he could just make out Greg sitting next to Sasha. The pair of them were chatting away. Lovely. 'No, he's here, he knows Leon the boxer apparently, so I can't bar him. Sarah's okay though.' Mad as hell at me for throwing her date out, but okay. Safe. 'I will get rid of them as soon as I can, I just don't want him turning up there after.'

'Okay son, don't worry. He won't get through the door. You had a good night otherwise?'

Rory thought of his date tonguing an Adonis in front of him. 'Dad, please just go there now. Drive safe though or take a taxi. If he sees your car he might just take a swing at it.'

'Ah, I think I'll take the car actually. Don't worry son, I'll be there faster than you think.'

The line clicked off and Rory relaxed a little. Bunny and Annabel would be okay, he would explain things to them later. And Sarah. Make her see why he had to get rid of Nigel. Although, seeing his reaction, he had as the kids say, 'done her a solid'.

He pocketed his phone, heading for the VIP area. Being a nice guy was so much easier than what he was trying to achieve now. He wondered what his mother would be thinking. He was trying to get a love life of his own, and he just seemed to be running around messing everyone else's up.

CHAPTER SEVENTEEN

Saturday night

Gill sat on the couch staring at his phone. He was in on his own for the first time in weeks, and he felt miserable. Dinah had decided to stay at home on her own for the first time, but it felt wrong for her to be there alone.

'I have to get used to it, Gill. My mum could be in hospital for months. She needs therapy for her stroke, and she's talking about going to a rehab centre, maybe not even coming home at all.' Elaine was in a bad way, they both know it. She was lucky to survive the massive stroke, but Gill knew it was more than that. Elaine had given up a long time ago. After her husband passed, and her son Elliott died, she had just not cared anymore. Dinah had spent her teens and twenties looking after her, taking her to the doctors for her depression, cleaning the house. Some days she had to bath her, feed her like a baby.

Gill's heart had broken more and more as she had opened up and told him about caring for her mother for so many years. How losing her dad and brother had sucked the life right out of her mother and put her own life on pause and rewind. Now it was even worse, and Dinah was alone in a house that looked like time had forgotten it. Gill was sat on his own in his bachelor pad of a house, nursing a beer and his own rather bruised ego. His pact with Rory to start dating following the plan was still on the starting blocks, and Rory was currently out with the woman of his dreams. The only thing Gill had managed to do was avoid his mother and the 'perfect date' she had set up ready. He had looked at a couple of dating sites, but the thought of actually putting himself out there, for others to pick over, was more than he could bear. He looked across at the television, where a man was dancing on a podium in a bow tie and shiny metallic pants. Modern dating shows nowadays. It wasn't about what an ideal date was, or their favourite colour. The days of Cilla Black were long gone. Nowadays it was naked dating, trials of fitness and dress sense, whether or not a bloke could tile a floor whilst sporting a perfect six pack and declaring everything to be 'sick'. Oh, and to be taken seriously, now you had to have manscaped eyebrows, no body hair and the type of tan that Donald Trump would be proud of. He felt like he wasn't in on something that the rest of the world was. Since when was reading books not cool, or even using the correct language? Sick to Gill conjured up images of snotty noses, cancer patients. Was he missing a memo or something? Things were not reem in Gill's world.

He went to get another bottle of beer from the fridge and looked in the hall mirror. He was dressed in blue denim jeans and a green Yoda t-shirt. He had a hairy chest, normal eyebrows without a tweeze in sight, and a thick mop of dark curls. His idea of a tan was far different to the day-glo buffed specimens on TV. He wasn't even sure he could tan, in all honesty. On every family holiday they had been on growing up, his mother had caked him in sun cream and the biggest sun hat she could find and stuck him in the shade. The only lad's holiday he had been on was to Blackpool on a disastrous stag do, and to go on a couple's break you needed to be in an actual couple. He realised that this was pathetic, but what to do? He spent his weekends at Cosplay conventions and conferences relating to accounting, when he wasn't holed up at home watching his favourite shows. He lifted his top up, showing off his flat stomach. He didn't have abs as such, but he did run every morning. Or had until recently. He looked at his running shoes, which were lined up neatly in the hallway. Maybe a Sunday morning run would be a good idea. He went to the kitchen, pulling a beer out of the fridge and popping off the cap with a Darth Vader bottle opener. He opened the drawer, pulling out the clipboard with his takeaway menus attached. If he was going to get back to his routine, he might as well have a blow out tonight. He heard his phone ring in the lounge, and he went to answer it, beer and clipboard in hand. He groaned when he saw the display.

'Hi Ma, how are you?' He sank down into the sofa and took a pull of his beer.

'I would be fine, if I had a son who cared about my happiness at all. Are you drinking?' Gill jumped up, snorting beer bubbles out of his nose.

'Ma, no,' he said, between coughs. He looked across at his bay window, where the curtains were open. He scanned outside, half expecting to see his mother hanging out of a bush with a pair of binoculars. He closed the curtains. 'I was going to call you back. I've been busy.'

'Busy ah? Doing what, ignoring your mother and festering in that big family free house you have?'

'No, actually I've been helping a friend. She's going through some stuff.'

'She? is this the girl you were talking about?'

Gill cursed himself for even telling his mother he was friends with a woman. Damn his loose tongue after a beer. 'Ah, er, no. That didn't work out. She's just a friend, she has a boyfriend anyway.'

'Is he Jewish?'

'Ma, what does that have to do without anything? I'm not dating him, am I? Listen, did you want something in particular or is this just a general pep talk?'

'Ira, will you hear how your son speaks to me? I never raised him this way. This is your fault.'

Gill heard the volume on the telly being raised at the other end, a few choice words from his father muttered. His mother squeaked in protest. 'Ira Cohen, how dare you watch that rubbish when our son needs us? Turn it off!'

He heard his mother switch hands with the phone, probably so she could get a better grip on his dad. They were like a bloody punch and Judy act.

'Mum! Ma!' He shouted into the phone to get her attention. 'Ma, I'm going.'

He could hear his dad shouting in the background. Something about missing Sanchez missing a goal and it being her fault for 'rabbiting on'. She came back onto the line, and he kept going. 'You're mad, woman, you know that! I told you, don't be bothering me with your matchmaking shenanigans when Arsenal's on!'

'Shut up, you old fart! Gill, I think it's time to set a date. There's a mixer at the community centre, the church has organised it for all the young people in the community. It's for people who haven't been matched yet, a way of meeting people. I signed you up. It's in a couple of weeks. I'll email you the details. I've told everyone you have a ticket now too, so don't be pulling out of it. I mean it Gill, if you embarrass me, I will never forgive you.'

Gill looked at the television screen, where a man was busily trying to stuff as many hot dog sausages into a girl's bra as he could to win a date with her. Maybe a night to meet other singles might not be the worst thing, even if his mother would be there.

'Okay Ma, send me the details. I'll go.'

There was silence on the line. 'Ma, I said I'll go.'

'I know what you said, I was just pinching myself. Glad you have finally seen the light. This will be the beginning of your life, Gill Cohen. You mark my words.'

He rang off, his mother positively happy at the news. At least his dad would get to watch Arsenal in peace. His mother would have gone into Def Con Three mode by now, ringing everyone in her circle of friends to tell them the news, co-ordinate outfits and plan the food she was going to take. If nothing else, he would be well fed. Everyone who attended these events all cooked their best dishes, not just to feed the guests, but as a way of outdoing each other. Since last year, Hyacinth's three tier prawn extravaganza was still talked about. Three of the families had ended up rioting in the car park, and Albert had lost the tip of his pinky finger in an unfortunate silver platter incident. He dialled Dinah's number, and she answered in two rings.

'Gill?' She sounded down, and he couldn't hear any other noise from the house.

'Dinah, you alone? Sorry, I know it's late.'

'Yes, I'm alone,' she said, 'I've been cleaning the house, though it doesn't really need it. I heard from Mum, the nurse phoned me. Social services have decided to put her in long term care. I'm going to sell the house, help her pay for it.'

Gill's heart broke for her. 'You want some company?'

CHAPTER EIGHTEEN

Monday morning

Greg walked into work like the cat that got the cream. All weekend he had been pretty smashed, and his hangover was pretty epic, but he still felt amazing. The look on Sarah's face when she had spotted him in the club said it all. She thought she was so good, so clever - like she could actually erase him from her life, just like that. It was comical. Sure, it had annoyed him at first. If there was one thing Greg hated, it was being told no. People acting like they were better than him. Like they had the upper hand. It just wasn't going to wash, and now she knew. She was beaten, fair and square.

He had gone to the club to see who was on that night. Maybe a change of staff might just let him slip through - then he could just sit at the end of the bar, quiet as a mouse, show her how he could get to her. Maybe pick up some tart to ruffle her feathers. Show her what she was missing by being pigheaded. When Leon Mendez had shouted across to him, he couldn't believe his luck. They had grown up together in the same part of Leeds, been to the same schools, the same watering holes, gyms. Greg had even saved Leon's nan from a chip pan fire in her kitchen a few years back. Shit like that bonded people, and Leon made a big fuss of him. Before he even had a chance to gloat, he was in. Sitting in the VIP area, getting his photo taken with Leon and his trainer. A hot red headed chick was hovering around, looking like she had just stepped off a catwalk.

'She with you?' he'd asked Leon, and Leon had winked at him

in reply.

'Nice eh?' he said, as they sat back on one of the plush sofas. 'She's my PR agent, Sasha.' Greg licked his lips as his gaze raked over her body. She was laughing with a couple of Leon's team, her giggles making her boobs jiggle in her dress. He looked across and found Sarah, who was busy serving customers in a club branded t-shirt and black trousers, hair pinned back from her face in a loose plait. She had always had a good figure, even after Annabel was born. She had never done much with it though, preferring the natural look. Maybe that was where he had gone wrong. Going for a woman who would rather study than get her nails done. Too much independence. Maybe he should try and pull this Sasha person, or one of the other groupies here. He nudged Leon, giving him the look of thanks and seeing that she had sat down, took the opportunity to sit next to her. She looked at him and smiled.

'Hey babe, you having a good night? Leon was saying you're a bit of a hero round here.'

Greg inwardly preened but made a good exterior show of brushing off her compliment. 'Ah, well - all in the day of a life of a fire fighter. Nothing major.' He fixed her with a 'I dare you not to drop your panties' look. 'The important thing is that I was there. It's the ones we don't get to that haunt me.'

Sasha's eyes widened, her pupils dilating. He moved closer to her. 'Fancy a drink?'

'Actually, Sasha has a drink, thank you, Greg.' A voice interrupted, and Sasha stood up to greet them.

'Rory, where have you been? I've been waiting for you, baby.' She leant forward and taking the cocktail from Rory's hands, she went in for a kiss. Rory deflected her a little, turning his face so that she got his cheek. She flinched, but soon recovered, motioning for Leon to join them.

'Leon, this is Rory Gallant, owner of Miranda's - he's in finance in the city.' She bopped her index finger on the edge of his nose. 'He's also my boyfriend, so be nice.'

Rory shook Leon's hand. 'Nice to finally meet you in the flesh, though I'm not -'

'Oh darling,' Sasha simpered. 'Don't be modest now. Rory here has his finger on the pulse, we can run more club nights here after the local fights. I know you said you wanted to branch out into mentoring, this could be beneficial for everyone, right?' She leaned into Rory, resting her head on his chest like a coy little girl. Leon whooped.

'Yeah, yeah! I can bring my new talent down, do paid meet and greets. Sasha, girl, you know your game!' He put his hand out to fist bump her, and she took it.

Greg stood up, fresh glass of bubbles in hand. 'Well, sound like you have a deal, eh Rory? I'm looking forward to coming to more nights like these, congratulations!' Leon patted him on the back.

'Yeah man, you're welcome to any night - free of charge. My treat. Bring your fire station buddies too. Boxers and firemen, we'll have our pick of the women.'

Greg laughed, a dirty laugh that made Rory's skin crawl. 'Oh, I don't have any problem getting women, do I Rory boy? Where's daddy-kins tonight, anyway?'

Rory felt Sasha's eyes on him. 'My father is not working tonight. I'll pass on your regards though.' He flicked his gaze to Sarah, she was still serving. Frankie was on with her, and Ian was standing at the end of the bar, looking at Greg as if he was a delectable snack. She was safe, and that was all that mattered tonight. The rest would just have to be endured.

'You do that,' Greg growled back. 'Or I'll tell him myself, next time I'm in.' The threat hung in the air between them, the words jabbing through the air like small pointed blades. Sasha, ever unobservant, started to chatter away to Leon and the others. Rory noticed the boxer's hand sliding up the small of her back. Nice Sasha, good talk. He made his excuses and headed over to the bar.

He went into the wash room and motioned to Frankie to send Sarah in. Frankie saluted him with two fingers together, and discreetly spoke to Sarah. Rory watched her through the window. She looked so tired and stressed as she slipped into the side room. 'I'm sorry, he had me over a barrel. Everyone's watching him, I'll talk to Sasha later, explain. He won't get in again.'

'I get it Rory, it's to keep the peace for the club, but what the hell was that with Nigel?' She spat at him. 'Why were you so rude? He did nothing wrong. And before you start, I am going to tell him about Annabel. I just wanted to check that he was worth telling first. What's the point of worrying about things like that before I have to? She already has that git in her life,' she jabbed her finger behind her at the door as her voice raised, 'I didn't see the point in complicating things. No point at all now though, since my 'boss' just threw him out!'

Rory ran his fingers through his hair in frustration. 'Sarah, I did that because Greg was in the club! I had to get him out before he saw you two together. I was trying to protect you, but in all honesty, the guy is a dick anyway. He basically told me how much of a dick he was himself. You can't see him anymore.'

Sarah exploded. 'I can't see him anymore! Who says? You? What the fuck does it have to do with you anyway, why do you feel the need to protect me all the time, Ror. I'm a grown woman!'

'Act like it then!' Rory shouted back. 'You keep picking these dirtbags! Why do you keep doing it to yourself, to Annabel?'

Sarah came forward, jabbing her fingers into Rory's chest. 'Greg is her dad, I didn't know he was like that till it was too late, but he gave me her! You can't expect me to regret that!'

'I don't! I love Annabel, you know that. I love you both!' They both stared at each other, wide eyed.

'Whatever that means,' she murmured after a beat.

'What?'

'What was that at the zoo then? Did you not think that we might have needed to talk about that? Or are you going to brush it under the carpet, as usual?'

Rory blinked hard, his mouth flapping open and closed as he tried to stutter out a response. 'Sarah, I don't want us to fall out. I...I'm trying.'

'Trying to do what, exactly? Do you have anything to say to me, or not?'

He waited a beat too long.

'I thought not,' she snorted. 'Come on, admit it Rory, you just want me to stay single, so you can come and play happy families whenever you want. You don't want me to be happy with anyone else, because that means you're alone. You never liked Greg!'

'This isn't about him!'

'No, it isn't but I'm right, aren't I?' They were openly shouting at each other now, faces and chests pushed close to each other.

'He's an arsehole! Damn right I didn't like him. You can do so much better. For god's sake Sar, don't you know how great you are?'

'Do you?' They both stared at each other, seeing their anger mirrored in each other's faces.

'Do I what?'

'See how great you are. That woman out there is horrible. She will never make you happy. She's the type of girl that you think you should like, because your dad does. You're nothing like your dad, but you're too stupid to see it. You could have any woman you wanted, if you just put yourself out there. It won't work with her, and you know it. She's a vapid leech, you don't have a thing in common with her!'

'You sound jealous.'

'Of her? Never. I would never be like her.'

'No,' Rory said, feeling an odd sensation in his chest. 'Jealous of her with me. You said I don't want you to be with anyone, what about you? You never liked Sasha either.'

Sarah shook her head. 'I despise her. She'll make you miserable.'

Rory opened his mouth to deny it, but the words stuck in his throat. 'Yeah, well I'm pretty miserable now, so what's the difference?' He pulled Tim's business card out of his trouser pocket. 'Tim from school wants to take you out. Call him.'

'How long have you had this?' She asked him, turning the card over and over in her hand.

'Does it matter?'

'Yes, it does!' She jabbed him in the chest. 'You had this

today, didn't you, and you didn't give it to me. Why, Rory? Or can't you work it out in that stupid oblivious head of yours?'

'Oh yeah, well you don't have seem to have things figured out either. Do us all a favour and pick a nice guy for once.' He strode across to the door. He felt so weird, so angry, shaky - he needed to get out of there. He didn't even know why he had put the card in his pocket.

'Oh,' he said as a parting shot. 'Nigel is barred from the club, so don't bring him here again. I'll go and get rid of Greg for you.'

She didn't answer, and he left. He felt better for about half a second before the crushing realisation that he had just taken a cheap shot sank in. He headed across to the VIP area. If Greg wanted to be given the VIP treatment, he would do just that.

Monday

Greg was still chuckling to himself as he clocked on. He was hoping that it would be a quiet Monday. He would make himself scarce till the school visits were all allocated, pretend to be cleaning in the back. The last thing he wanted to do today was go and talk to a school full of screaming, excited children about fire safety. He was due to don the mascot outfit too. With the alcohol sweats in full flow the last thing he needed was to sweat it out in a fox outfit as Freddie the Firefighter Fox. Plus, the thing never got washed and stank of butt crack and stale farts.

'Greg, can I have a word please?' The station chief appeared around the corner.

Greg rolled his eyes and turned back to the chief, putting on his best professional face. 'Morning Chief, of course you can. I was just about to get on with the cleaning. We have a lot of laundry to do today too, and young minds to shape.'

Chief Carrington cleared his throat, his face not even cracking a smile. 'Don't worry about that for now Greg, just come to my office, okay?'

Greg followed him through to his office. A woman in a sharp navy suit sat on one of his chairs, facing his desk. Chief Carrington went behind his desk and sat down.

'Come in Greg and shut the door.'

He did as he was asked, wincing as the sound of the heavy door closing banged in his throbbing head.

'This is April, from HR. I'm afraid that there has been a complaint made against you. A member of the community has brought to our attention that you have been drinking, causing fights, and harassing one of their staff. Apparently, you were barred from the establishment, but you went back more than once. What do you have to say on the matter?'

That little bitch. She reported me! 'Listen Chief, this is all one big misunderstanding. It's not what you think, I've had a bit of a disagreement with my girlfriend. She works there, and she's obviously still a bit mad at me. It won't happen again, I'm trying to sort it out. We have a daughter together, we're a family.' He did his best 'my woman is mad' face at the Chief, but his face remained stony.

He could feel the woman's eyes boring into the side of his head, so he didn't even try to sneak a peek with her. Women stuck together, everyone knew that. He had already lost with her.

'Is that your official answer, that it's just a domestic disagreement? You weren't barred for your behaviour, or drunk and disorderly?'

Greg looked suitably horrified. 'Chief, you know me. Of course not!'

Carrington folded his arms across his chest and puffed his cheeks out. 'April, help me out here.'

The woman turned to him. 'These are very serious charges Greg. We believe that you have been harassing certain people at a local establishment and have been threatening and violent. We also believe that you may have been hungover on a few shifts lately, to the extent where your colleagues themselves raised concerns about your ability to fulfil your work duties. Are you drunk now, Greg?'

Greg jumped up, causing his chair to skitter across the floor. 'How dare you! I am a respected part of this house!'

'Sit down, Greg!' The Chief boomed. 'I can smell the alcohol on you from here. The lads are not happy, they're not willing to work with you anymore. We have been sent CCTV evidence of you verbally abusing a business owner, and people are willing to give statements about your behaviour. I have had an allegation of harassment and violence against the mother of your child! You are done!'

'Chief,' April warned. 'We have protocols, remember?'

'Oh yes, yes, I know.' He waved her away, visibly angry at the situation. 'I'm going to leave, let you sort out -' he glared at Greg. 'This.' He stood up, striding out of the office and slamming the door behind him. Greg turned to look at April, and she looked down her nose at him, her lips set into a thin line.

'Shall we get started, or would you like to contact your union representative first?'

Greg scowled and sagged in his chair.

CHAPTER NINETEEN

Dinah woke up to the sound of her phone ringing. She went to turn the button off, thinking it was her alarm and ended up swiping to answer the call. A voice sounded out in the silence of the neat and tidy room.

'Dinah? Dinah? Answer me, I mean it. Stop doing this!'

She pushed her elbows down on the mattress and hauled herself up in the fresh cream sheets. She held the phone to her ear and took a deep breath. 'Eric, hi.'

'Are you frigging kidding me? Dinah, I've been calling you for weeks and got the brush off. You barely ever answer, you don't let me see you. I called your work, left messages. What the hell is going on? I demand to know what's wrong with you. We have Leeds Comicon in three weeks, we were supposed to co-ordinate our costumes, remember? What the hell is going on, and where is your mother? Every time I drive past the house it's either in darkness or the curtains are shut. Is she not well?'

Dinah took a deep breath. She owed him the truth. In all honesty, she thought he would have just stopped calling by now. They weren't serious, and he didn't seem the type to hang outside a girl's bedroom window with an ipod speaker held above his head. 'You phoned work? What did they say?'

'They wouldn't tell me anything, since you never mentioned me there. They didn't believe I could be your boyfriend, so they told me that you were on leave and to stop calling. What's going on?'

'My mother had a stroke,' she pushed out on a shaky breath. The words ripped through her like a knife, and she winced at the pain. 'She's never been right since Elliott died.' Died snorting enough drugs to fell an elephant. Died young, leaving her to pick up the pieces. 'She hasn't been looking after herself. I tried to help her, but...she had a massive stroke. She's in a rehabilitation centre. She's decided to stay there.'

'I'm so sorry Dinah. You should have told me, I would have been there for you. Listen, your mother is probably in the best place. Like you said, she's never been right. Maybe you can start to live a little now, for yourself. What's er...what's going to happen with the house?'

'The house?' Dinah echoed.

'Well yeah, is it yours now?'

Dinah laid in bed looking up at the painted ceiling of Gill's guest room and listened to the sound of Eric breathing into her ear. Of all the information he could have zeroed in on, it was the house. He hadn't asked where she had been when she wasn't at home, or if he could see her, or do anything to help. He had chosen to focus on the house, and suddenly it all clicked into place. 'Tell me Eric, if we didn't have Leeds Comicon coming up, would you have bothered to track me down like this? You could have found me really. Did you ever leave a note at my house, or knock on the door? Did you call any of my friends? Do you even remember the names of any of them? I have Mum's phone, and you never tried to call that.'

Suddenly she was seeing their relationship in new light. The meals she paid for, the nights she had spent sat on her own while he went out with clients, work colleagues. She was always just on the fringes of his life, like a child's occasional plaything. The man had money, and never seemed to really work for it. As a nurse and a carer, she had to work for everything she had. The thought of him sniffing around her mother's house, especially while she was still alive, made her feel sick. She heard the sound of footsteps outside her door, and Gill's soft knock.

'Dinah, you up? I'm going to put some coffee on, okay?'

'Who was what?' Eric asked, his voice high pitched. 'Was that...was that Gill? Why is Gill at your house this early?'

She ignored him, covering her phone with her hand. 'Morning Gill, I'll be there in two. I'm just making a call.'

'Okay,' called Gill breezily, and she heard him head down the stairs. He was humming the theme song from Star Wars, and it made her giggle. He always made her happy. He made her happy and got nothing in return. He never asked her for a thing, besides her company.

'Listen Eric,' she said sweetly. 'Mum is selling the house to pay for her care. Do you think we should perhaps get somewhere together? We talked about it before.'

Eric spluttered down the phone, making a sound like a child pretending to fire a gun. An 'er er er' sound, like a bleating sheep. 'Er, well we can talk about that when we meet up to go over the costumes. I'm not sure it's the best idea, to move in quite yet. Doesn't the house come to you now anyway? You should get a solicitor, check it out.'

'Whip the house out from under my mother now, you mean?' she said caustically. The barb missed Eric down the line somehow.

'Yeah, see if she can transfer it or something. That way, you have your future set.' He droned on, oblivious to the sarcasm in her tone. 'Our future. A lick of paint, and that place could be a good family home.'

That does it. 'Eric, it is a good family home. MY family home, my parents raised my brother and I there, and it might be tatty and outdated, but it was my home all my life. Sometimes you have to let go and move on.'

'Well, yes, I suppose. Actually, one of the new builds on the new estate could be nice, shall I get some brochures? We could go at the weekend, they do part exchange.'

'By letting go Eric, I mean you. My mother is selling her house to pay for her care, and I'm moving on. I'm starting my own life for once, and part of that means getting the hell away from you.' She threw the covers back, her anger necessitating her need to pace up and down the room in her long t-shirt and Wonder Woman panties. 'Do you know what? I could kill you. I should have realised how I felt when I didn't want to call you for help. The truth was, I can't rely on you. Or even want you there with Mum. You've strung me along for months, and all you care about is yourself and how much stuff you've got. Why would I fleece my own mother to finance a life with you? You really are the biggest, stupidest, most clueless, idiotic knobhead I have ever had the misfortune to meet. You can sew your own damn costumes from now on, and just as a suggestion, why don't you just go as yourself - an arsehole!'

She threw the phone onto the bed and headed out of the room. She arrived in the kitchen, panting with the remnants of the anger she had just expelled. She felt great.

Gill turned to look at her when she walked in, and he blushed furiously. 'Er, morning. Everything okay?' He was looking at her oddly, his eyes moving up and down her body, and she realised with a jolt she was wearing her WW pants and one of his Supernatural t-shirts. She tugged the hem down embarrassed.

'Oh God, I'm so sorry,' she mumbled. 'I wasn't thinking.'

Gill put down the mug he had been holding and taking his dressing gown off, moved towards her. He put it around her shoulders. She caught a whiff of his aftershave and mint toothpaste as he folded it over her. She made no move to wrap the cord around herself and felt him sneaking a further peek.

'It's okay, I've never seen Jensen Ackles look better,' he smirked, referring to the actor's face that was emblazoned across her breasts. He blushed again, and she reached out to touch his cheek. He didn't move, but she heard him take a deep breath in.

'Everything okay with your mum?' He breathed, looking concerned once again.

'Did you hear the call?'

'Some of it. Sorry, I wasn't prying. I just wanted to know you were okay.'

She looked at him, her friend, her curly haired Gill. His sci-fi geekiness matched hers perfectly. He never asked for a thing but was always there. He was such a nice guy, and she suddenly acknowledged what she should have seen all along.

'I fancy you, Gill Cohen.' She raised her hand to meet the other, holding his face between them. 'You never ask for anything, and you are always there. Do you know why I didn't call Eric, when my mum was taken ill?'

Gill's eyes were sparkling now, and he shook his head gently.

'I didn't call Eric because he never even entered my head. I instinctively called you, I wanted and needed you with me. I never realised that properly, not till now.'

Gill smiled then, a happy goofy smile that she returned. 'Stay with me,' he said softly. 'I'll help you sell your mum's house, but don't go live alone somewhere. Stay here, with me. We don't have to do anything, you can sleep in the -'

She cut him off by kissing him. She moved closer to him, feeling his body against her thin t-shirt. He responded instantly, kissing her back and holding her tight. They kissed feverishly, till Gill broke the kiss.

'What about Eric?' he said, his face looking panicked. 'You're with Eric.'

Dinah laughed, kissing him again once. 'I dumped him this morning. Why didn't you tell me he was a complete arsehole?'

Gill laughed. 'I tried. I was trying to be a gent.'

Dinah kissed him again, harder this time. 'Well, this little lady wants to go back to bed. You coming?'

Gill grinned boyishly, and she felt a pang of passion stir within her. He pretended to tip an imaginary hat at her and scooped her up into his arms. She squealed and giggled.

'Madam, your wish is my command.'

CHAPTER TWENTY

Wednesday

4 weeks later

Sarah walked out of the solicitor's office and headed across the small park that formed the centre of Park Square. Looking at the clock tower, she realised that she could make her afternoon lecture after all, and she started to walk up to university. She opened her oversized bag and stuffed the thick envelope full of papers into its depths, pulling out her mobile phone.

'Hello darling, I can't really talk long. I'm just on a break from my class. Everything go okay?'

Sarah walked into a small sandwich shop and waited in line. 'Well, it's not going to be cheap, but I can just about pull it off. The solicitor said I can pursue him for the costs, and for maintenance, but I'm not going to. I just want him gone. She's filing for a custody hearing and a residence order and prohibited steps order is going through.'

Bunny went quiet, and Sarah could hear her whispering, the line muffled. 'Mum, did you hear me? Shall I call you later?'

'No love, it's fine. I was just asking someone what all that meant.'

'Mum,' Sarah retorted, lowering her own voice. 'I don't really like the idea of you telling every tom dick and harry about my car wreck of a life, if you don't mind.'

'Doug's not nobody, love.'

'Doug?' Sarah said out loud, drawing the stares of the queue of hungry grey lunchtime workers. 'Why is Doug at pottery class?'

'Doug isn't at pottery class, dear.' She said this as though she was speaking to a forgetful idiot. 'It's life drawing on a Wednesday.' She tittered, and Sarah looked at the phone in her hand to check it was actually her mother she was speaking to, not some crank caller. 'You should sign up, it's really rather fun.' Her mother's voice dropped by a whisper. 'I'm sat looking at a penis! When's the last time you did that?' The man in front of Sarah in the queue emitted a short burst of laughter, and she cursed today's modern day phones. You might as well be on speakerphone, the way the sound rang out. Especially with the gob on her mother, whose idea of being discreet was a stage whisper.

'Mother! Look, I have to go. I'll talk to you later, okay?'

'Okay, and don't forget, I can't get Annabel today. I told her you would be collecting her.'

Sarah cursed. 'What, since when?'

'It's on the fridge dear, I left a note.'

Sarah thought back to that morning - she didn't remember seeing it on the calendar. Bollocks. She was supposed to be studying in the library at pick up time. 'Okay, okay. No problem, I'll get her. I can work from home later.'

Her mother was already chatting away in the background, presumably to Doug, judging from his easy laugh. 'You could call Rory, you know. I'm sure he would love to pick Annabel up. He hasn't seen her for a while, and she misses him.'

Sarah hung up on her mother, shoving the phone into her bag.

The man turned around to look at her.

'You want a picture?'

The man shuffled forward in the line, tutting to himself. She looked at the clock tower again. She might as well go to her lecture now, get there early and try and get some work done before it started. She ignored her growling belly and headed out of the shop.

Rory sat in the hotel bar, nursing his soft drink as he waited for Sasha. They had planned a lunch date, but as usual Sasha couldn't just rock up to a country pub and have a carvery lunch or call into Pizza Express. She had to have a posh lunch out, somewhere she could be seen, be photographed. Collect more photos for her album of a food diary. In the last month, her Insta feed looked more like a restaurant menu than a snapshot of life. Rory had always thought that her social media was for the good of her firm, but she was like this all the time. It was all getting a little bit wearing. Sasha Birkenstock seemed to be all smoke, gloss and mirrors. He kept looking for hidden depths, like looking beneath the surface of the ocean at the wonders underneath, but truth was, she was more like a puddle.

'Hey,' she said as she sidled into the seat next to him. 'Hi Gary, Grey Goose for me, please.'

The bartender smiled. 'No problem Sasha. Right away.' He looked in question at Rory, but he shook his head.

'No thanks, I'm fine.' He looked at Sasha who was busy checking her lipstick. 'Thanks for coming to meet me.'

She dropped a kiss onto his lips. 'Of course, shall we get a table?'

Rory looked at his watch, it was nearly half one already. 'I can't sorry, I have a meeting later. I just really wanted to talk to you about something.'

Sasha winked at the bartender and took a sip of her drink.' Thanks Gary, put it on my tab, okay?'

Gary nodded, staring doe eyed at her will Rory cleared his throat pointedly. 'Yes, thanks Gary. That will be all.' Sasha jabbed him in the side.

'What?' he said irritably.

'You, being grumpy, again. I have contacts here.'

'You have contacts everywhere. Anyway, listen about the boxing, last month. It's been bugging me for a while, and I just think we need to talk about it.'

Sasha groaned like a petulant teenager. 'For God's sake Rory, I told you, the Leon thing doesn't mean anything. It's just business. A bit of fun. Can we forget about it already? You've been snippy about this for weeks!'

Rory ran one hand through his hair, trying to resist the urge he felt to rip it out at the roots. It would be more pleasurable than this conversation, that's for sure. 'I don't care about Leon, well I do, you know I don't like that, but I mean Greg.'

Sasha pulled a face. 'Greg, the fireman? I didn't kiss him. Did I?'

Rory looked at her open mouthed. She was seriously asking him to tell her. Did she not remember who she swopped saliva with in the last month? 'Are you really asking me that question?'

Another eye roll. 'Yes Rory, I was. I like to have fun sometimes, unlike some. The bubbles sometimes make me a bit wild, nothing major. We did agree that this was resolved though, right? No kissing anyone else?'

'Right. Yes. Well, whatever. Fine. About Greg-'

'The fireman.'

'Yes, Greg the fireman. I can't have him in the club anymore, he's barred from the premises.'

'For kissing me?'

Rory gritted his teeth and held his breath for a few seconds. 'No, you just said he didn't kiss you.'

'Well, he didn't.'

'Good, not barring him for it then, am I?'

Sasha smiled, clinking her glass against his. 'All sorted then! Was that it, do you want to get some lunch?'

Rory pinched the top of his nose between two fingers. He could feel himself getting angry. The woman had an attention span of a goldfish! He looked across at her, and as usual she was totally oblivious to his mood. The conversation was already forgotten in her mind, if she even remembered it in the first place. How could he spend time with this woman? What would she do, doll their children up like pet projects, give them awful names? She was taking a selfie with her cocktail. He saw her type the hashtags #humpdayfeals #workinghard and his blood ran cold. She hadn't even spelt feels correctly. All of a sudden, he had a flash of his future. Him, older like his dad, medallion swinging from his half open shirt, swaggering around his club like Peter G -string.

He could see it now, his wedding in Hello magazine surrounded by her clients, their children decked out in designer bling, called unique names like Gif or Cloud. Or even Hashtag. He shuddered inwardly.

'Sasha, I can't see you anymore. I'm sorry.'

She tilted her phone to him. 'I can see you, look!' She pouted her lips and took a selfie of the two of them, him looking very bemused indeed. 'Oh, that's not the best.' She frowned and looked genuinely upset. 'I'll put a filter on it.'

Rory reached for the phone and set it face down on the bar. 'Look at me, Sasha. I'm telling you that I don't want to see you anymore. It's not working out. I'll still host any events you want at the club, I'll keep it professional. Greg the fireman is barred. He's a horrible man. If he comes to the club again, he'll be arrested. It's nothing to do with you, but I would advise you to keep your clients away from him. He's bad news.'

She didn't say anything, just looked at him blankly.

'Sasha, did you hear what I said?'

She moved her head once, flipping her hair back from her face. 'I heard you, yes. I'm just not sure I've ever heard it before. You're saying this is over?'

Rory smiled kindly. 'I'm sure you haven't. You're great really, but we are from very different worlds. I'm a geeky accountant, and I set out to act like a person I thought you wanted. It worked for a while, but then I realised that I don't like this person. I liked the old me. I just need to find someone who does too.'

He peeled off a note from his wallet and set it on the bar. 'Give me a call about your next event. I would hate the club to miss out on your business because of me. My dad built that business from the ground up, and it works well. Take care of yourself, Sasha.'

He squeezed her shoulder gently and started to walk away.

'Rory?' She called after him.

'Yes?'

She gave him one of her million dollar smiles. 'The girl behind the bar. I think she might be the one you're looking for.' Rory looked at her aghast. She raised a brow at him. 'Listen, I might be a little self obsessed, but I know a girl in love when I see one. The question is, when are you going to wake up to it?'

He stood frozen to the spot. Was that true? He thought of how angry he had gotten with Nigel, and Greg. Sure, he had warned them both off, but they were basically pond sucking amoeba. He was just protecting his friend. She didn't love him, either. Hell, at the minute she wasn't even speaking to him. The whole thing was a joke. Sasha was way off. He noticed that she was still watching him.

'What, in denial?' It sounded mocking, but he could see she was being sincere. 'Or scared to admit it? I might not know the real Rory, but I know enough to know that he's not a coward.' Maybe she did have hidden depths after all. She spotted someone behind him and grabbed her phone. 'Bye Rory. I'll give you a call.'

The moment gone, she tottered off to greet someone coming through the hotel doors. Probably someone who would end up paying for lunch and feel privileged and lucky to do so. He watched her work the room. She really was a sight to behold. She would make some guy very happy one day. For Rory though, some dreams were better left there, the reality was what he really craved.

Rory slipped out. He had an appointment to get to, and he was never late. Some things about the old Rory had never truly gone.

Pulling up near the school an hour or so later, Rory turned off his engine and steadied a breath. This was it. This was his chance. He looked across at the flowers on his passenger seat, and Annabel's car seat in the back. He hadn't been able to stop thinking about what Sasha had said as he left, and the truth was, he was curious. Maybe their fall outs lately were more than just friends having a fight. Maybe Sarah was feeling odd about it too. Was that what she meant at the zoo? Was she really telling him that? He needed to see her, now - work out his feelings for himself. He had missed her so much, and not speaking every day to her had killed him. Was that just friendship? Today was supposed to be a chance to see her, to make it up. When Bunny had called him to ask him to step in and pick Annabel up, he had jumped at the chance. Bunny had classes all day, followed by one in the evening. She wouldn't be home till late. Rory could drop Annabel off, give Sarah the flowers, make friends again. These last few weeks had been so weird, and not speaking to her at all was torture. He didn't even know what he was going to say. He was hoping the words would come when he saw her. They usually did. Since primary school, bonding over the loss of a parent, they had found each other and been as thick as thieves ever since. Having things to say to Sarah was never a problem. Even after Greg came on the scene, they were still strong. Still best friends. He loved Annabel like she was his own child, and the more he thought of another Nigel or even a Tim coming along and taking them both away from him, the more his chest constricted. He needed to talk to her. Figure it out. He'd tried Gill but there had been no answer on his mobile. The office receptionist, a new hire to help with the workload, had said he was working remotely for the day. That was their code for 'something happened, and I can't come in. Leave me be.' So, he'd done just that.

He left the car and headed to the school gates. He spotted Lee in the crowd.

'Hey, man!' Lee said, greeting him with a too hard slap on the back. 'What are you doing here?'

He could see Tim a few feet away, back turned to them, talking to a woman. 'I came to pick Belle up. Bunny and Sarah have classes today.'

Lee pointed at Tim. 'Isn't that Sarah?'

He saw her then, talking to Tim. They looked cosy, stood close together as she chatted away aside from the usual gaggles of waiting parents. He laughed at something she said, and Rory's heart squeezed. He was normally the one making her laugh. Lee nudged him.

'Hey man, don't worry about it. She never called him, so he's just taking his shot probably.'

'She didn't call him?' He double checked. Lee shrugged.

'Nah mate, he never heard from her. I assume you gave her the card?'

Rory nodded miserably, thinking back to the fight in the wash room. 'Not my finest hour, I can tell you.' They hadn't spoken since then. She'd ignored his calls, only spoke to him about work through the staff. She had even emailed him about the stock for the bars, when he was sitting in the office two feet away from her. He didn't know how to make it right. She needed to apologise too, but there was no sign of that. It was definitely where Annabel got her stubbornness from.

'Rory, if you wanted to ask her out yourself, you shouldn't have given her the number in the first place. Do you like her?'

Rory looked back at the two parents, who were now standing

side by side talking as they watched the doors for their children to come spilling out. They look good together. He was a good guy. He would look after her, be a good dad.

'Yes,' he said sadly. 'I do. I actually think I love her.' He didn't wait for Lee's reply, he walked away. Heading for his car, he ignored Lee calling after him and drove away. As he checked his mirrors, his eyes fell on the car seat in the back of the car, the flowers on the seat next to him. He drove around for a while, avoiding going home for the evening. There was no point going back to the office, the club was shut, and all that was waiting for him at home was a few cans of beer and the television. He kept driving, numbly gathering his thoughts as he drove. Trying to shake the image of Sarah at school. He hadn't got the chance to see Annabel either. He wondered whether Bunny had told her he was supposed to collect her. He hated the thought of her looking for him at the classroom door, but he had to get out of there. Sarah had made it quite clear recently what she thought of his attempts to meddle in her love life. Bringing it to school would make it even worse. It was some time later, when the sky was just getting dark, that he realised where he was. He recognised the street, although he hadn't been for a while. Not since Dad stopped taking him as a teenager. It had never occurred to him to come on his own. He pulled into the parking place at the side of the road and turned off the engine. Taking the flowers, he locked up the car and walked over to the heavy metal gates. Pushing his way through, he headed to where she was. Her plot was under the shade of a tree, facing a memorial bench at the bottom. It was set apart from the others, in a little corner of its own. He placed the flowers in a water urn next to her headstone, noticing that there was a set of blooms already there, maybe a couple of days old. He read the card.

To my wife, it read. Love you always, Doug and Rory

He put the card back in place. The grave was well tended, not a weed in sight, and Rory wondered whether his father did that too. He stood up, taking a seat on the bench. The light was fading a little, the reddish pink sunset making its presence known on the horizon. It was so peaceful here, Rory could hear the leaves rustle in the trees nearby, the birds singing to each other. She would have loved it.

'Hi Mum,' he said, looking at the stone fondly, tears welling in his eyes. 'I see Dad's been coming. I bet he's always been hasn't he, even when I left and went to uni?'

He thought of all the years that stretched out from that day to this, all the things he had done and seen. She hadn't been there for any of it, and his heart broke at the thought. She'd never see his kids, be the mother of the groom weeping in the aisle. She would always be a space in the family photographs. A void.

'I'm sorry I haven't been for a long time. I'd like to say I've been busy, but I haven't really. I've been playing it safe, and the one time I don't follow your advice it all blows up in my face.' He wiped a tear from his cheek with the back of his hand. 'Sarah has a daughter now you know. Annabel. She's nearly seven. You'd love her, she's just like Sarah. I wish you could have met them. Dad and I are getting on better too, I've been working with him actually, at Miranda's. It's nice. I wish I hadn't been such an angry kid all these years, we missed out on a lot.'

The flowers moved with the wind, the cellophane making a crinkling noise that broke the silence. 'I've messed up, Mum. I didn't see it, and now it's too late. I don't even know if she likes me that way, but I can't even ask her now. I can't interfere in her love life again.'

His phone rang in his pocket, and he looked at the screen, sniffing loudly. He looked at the gravestone. 'If this is your doing, Mum, thanks.' He looked back at the screen, where a photo of Sarah and Annabel posing with a monkey at the zoo was lit up.

'Hi Sarah, thanks for calling.'

'Rory, could you come over please? It's Annabel. She's gone missing.' He could hear the worry in her voice. 'Please Rory, I don't know where to look. I went to put some clothes away upstairs, and when I came down, she was gone. The back door was wide open. Rory, please, I need you.'

Rory was already on his feet, running to the car. 'I'm on my way. Ring the police. Stay there. I'm here, Sar, I'm coming.'

He raced to his car, dialling his dad as soon as she hung up. His dad answered jovially. 'I'm in a phallic art class son, can I call you back?'

Rory slammed his driver door shut, throwing his phone into the cradle the second the car kit picked it up. He drove off at speed, racing to get to Sarah. 'Annabel's gone missing, Dad, from home. Sarah's ringing the police. Can you come? Ring the club, see if anyone has seen Greg too. He'll be pissed off about his job. Can you ring Bunny?'

Doug's tone changed instantly, back to brisk business man mode. 'Bunny dear, we have to go home. Annabel's missing.'

'Bunny's with you?' Rory asked. 'Why? What the hell is a phallic art class?'

Doug cut him off. 'I'll tell you all that later. We're on our way.'

The line clicked off and Rory concentrated on driving,

slowing his speed when he neared town. Hordes of schoolkids were out, still walking home, playing in the park, and he searched their faces for hers as he drove past. She never left the house alone, she knew better. She was far too smart for that. Someone had to have taken her. He waited till he hit a straight road and put his foot down.

The police cars were already there when Rory pulled up. Two officers were just getting out of the car, and one of them looked at him warily, putting his hand on his belt and motioning for the female officer accompanying him to knock on the door.

'Sir, can I help you?' Rory went to run past him to the house, but the officer put his hand out. 'Stop please Sir, show me some ID.'

'What? I need to - oh right, I'm not Greg. I'm Sarah's -'

'Rory!' She shouted, half sobbing on the doorstep. Rory pulled out his driving licence card, thrusting it at the officer. He nodded and moved his hand, Rory racing to the door. He pulled Sarah into his arms.

'Shhh, it's ok, listen, your mum's on her way. Dad's bringing her. Did you ring Greg?'

'I tried. It just goes to voicemail. I think he switched it off.' She pulled away and looked at him, teary eyed. 'Do you think he's got her? She wouldn't just leave, surely? She knows better. Why would he do it? I went to the solicitors today, I filed papers against him for her, but I doubt he got them yet. I don't even think they're legally binding yet.'

Rory's face fell. 'Where's her passport?'

'I have it, it's still upstairs, I checked.' The female officer came into the room, carrying a tray full of tea cups when the male officer came in.

'We've spoken to Greg Beckett. He has been at his mother's house all day. She and a neighbour verified it. He's intoxicated, showed up there late last night and still hasn't got up.'

Typical, thought Rory. The useless git was sleeping off a bottle of scotch, and his daughter was missing. 'At least he hasn't got Annabel,' Rory said to a trembling Sarah.

'Rory, that's not good though is it? Because as bad as that would be, at least she would be okay with him. Anyone could have her!' She covered her mouth with her hands, trying to stop the hysterical noises that were coming out of her own body. 'I can't take this, I can't!'

She went to stand up, and the phone rang. Everyone stilled, and there was a commotion at the door. The male officer went to deal with that while the female officer stood next to Sarah. 'Stay calm and answer the phone.'

'Hello? Annabel?' Sarah said into the receiver. 'Jane? Hi - listen I can't really - she is? Oh my God, thank you. Thank you! Is she okay?' Her face sagged with relief and she sank back into Rory's arms. 'Okay, we'll be right there. Don't let her leave, please!' She put the phone back in its cradle. 'She's ok, she's at the library. Jane said she's sitting where we normally do, writing in a notebook.'

Doug and Bunny walked into the room and Bunny went to hug her daughter. 'Oh, my darling, that is good news. I can't tell you how frantic we've been on the way here. You go and get her, Doug and I will make some food. I bet she's starving.'

Rory and Sarah went to leave.

'Dad?' he said, turning back to Doug.

'Yes, son?' Doug replied, tea tray in hand.

'Thanks for being here. I don't give you enough credit for what you do. I never have.'

Doug smiled broadly. 'It's my job, son.'

Rory went to shake his hand but threw his arms around him instead. 'I went to see Mum today. Thanks for looking after her all this time.' Doug said nothing, squeezing him tighter. 'Oh, and we're going to talk later about the fact that you and Bunny are obviously seeing each other, too.'

Doug chuckled. 'That's fine son, we've nothing to hide.'

Sarah threw off her coat and walked over to the reading area. Jane left them alone, trundling off with a trolley full of books. Rory stood in the doorway, talking to the officers who had followed them to check on the child.

'Annabel?' Her mother called to her. She was expecting a hug, a big reunion, she had it in her head on the way over that they would fling their arms around each other, overjoyed to be reunited. What she got was a peeved stare from her only child. 'Annabel, why did you go? I didn't have a clue where you were, we called the police. Your nana was frantic.'

'I went because I didn't want to be at home anymore. I still don't want to come home.'

'Why not? Is it your dad?'

Annabel shook her head. 'No, I don't want to see him anyway. I had a plan, and you spoiled it.'

Rory came and sat down next to them. 'Hey, Belle.'

Her face lit up when she saw him, and she jumped into his

arms. 'Rory, why didn't you stay at home time?'

Sarah looked at Rory questioningly. 'You were at school today? Why?'

'I told you Mum, we had a plan. Nana asked him to pick me up, and I was going to tell you the plan, but then you were talking to one of the other dads, and Rory got sad and left.'

Rory looked at the floor, feeling his face flush. Outed by a six year old. She must have seen the whole thing.

'What is she talking about? You came and left because I was speaking to Tim?'

'Er, well, Bunny asked me to pick Belle up, and I wanted to talk to you about something. I bought you some flowers to apologise, but I gave them to Mum instead.'

'You bought me flowers? You went to see your mum?'

'Yes, are you going to let me tell you, or are you going to keep repeating what I say?'

Sarah folded her arms, sticking her tongue into the inside of her cheek.

'I came to tell you that I think I figured out why.' He looked at Belle, who was sitting on his lap hanging on his every word.

'We should talk about this later, let's get Belle home.'

'No!' Annabel said, shimmying out of his grasp and reaching for the notebook. 'It's my plan, see?' She opened the book and Rory and Sarah looked at the pictures. Belle stopped on their graduation photo, the one in the crayon love heart.

'Annabel, where did you get all these photos from?'

'Nana's albums. I don't want to see Dad. I want to be a family together, me, you, Nana, and Rory.'

Rory picked Annabel up and passed the notebook to Sarah. ‘Well, your nana is cooking tea, so let's start with getting you fed and warm.’ He headed to the car, his mind racing. Annabel wanted them to be together. Another reason to tell her how he felt, but would it hurt Annabel if it didn't work out? He never wanted to go through anything like today again. He was willing to take the risk, but was it too great? If they didn't work out, if she didn't feel the same, he could lose them all. He couldn't bear that.

Behind him, Sarah was flicking through the notebook at the photos. Annabel had listed things about her, about Rory. She had written detailed notes about why they would be good together. For a six year old it was both endearing and terrifying. The person who Annabel chose to fall in love with would be so lucky but would need to be strong as hell. Just like Rory was with her. He had never once let her down. Even when she thought he wasn't, he was out there protecting her. As a friend though. He wanted Sasha, not her. She closed the book and followed them out.

CHAPTER TWENTY-ONE

Friday

Greg Beckett had finally made it. It had been a little hairy back then, sure, but he had come shooting out of the other side like a rocket ship. He couldn't wait to see the finished result. Screw being a fireman. He didn't need their suspensions, or their unpaid leave. Screw the Chief and his anger management. He had been given a month's suspension and couldn't even turn on a tap at the fire house till he had finished his course on how to manage his feelings. What did they want him to do all that time? Frigging meditate? He had been pounding bag instead, with Leon Mendez, and now he had his very own career to look forward to. He was back at the station next week, albeit behind a desk. He couldn't wait to rub his new side venture into their snobby fat faces. He couldn't believe his luck when Sasha had called him. Alongside her PR work, she'd decided to do a charity calendar for local businesses, in conjunction with Leon. A calendar. He had been trying to organise one at the station for ages, but the lads were all under the thumb and didn't want to get involved. They were all scared of their wives and girlfriends and how they would react. Set of pussies. Eventually the chief had vetoed the idea, but this was even better. He had spent the day dressed up in sexy fire gear, posing with props, oiled up. He had loved every minute of it, and not only that, he was going to be Mr July. Only the hottest guys got the warm summer months. The munters always got the cold ones. Mr January never got the love from the women buying the calendars. The only downside was the fee. The people sitting for the calendars hadn't been paid, they did it for the charitable donations the calendar would raise. He hadn't been best pleased when he heard that, but what was he gonna do? Leon was involved. He needed to ride this gravy train as long as he could, and this was a first step. Sasha had been great though, signing him as a client. She said he had potential, and he had signed away the rights to the photos from the day. She said she was going to get him some modelling work off the back of them, and she had come through.

Now here he was, heading into the offices of his agent, his PR person, to pick up a fat cheque. He wished Sarah could see him now. Since he got served with the papers, he hadn't been allowed to contact her. If he wanted to see his own daughter, he had to go to some contact centre, be monitored, watched over while he spent time with his own kid. As if. Greg didn't need parenting lessons from some stuck up cow who probably didn't even have kids herself because she couldn't get anybody to sleep with her in the first place. Busy bodies, the lot of them. Well, Sarah wanted him to pay for his kid and not see her? Not a chance in hell. She would have to take him to court first, and he wasn't even earning at the minute, being on unpaid suspension and then half pay desk duty bullshit. Good luck to her. He would be fine, he would just move back in with his mum if he needed to. He was going to ask Sasha to write that cheque out to his mother too, as a proxy. That way she couldn't get her hands on it. Why should Sarah have a penny of his hard earned modelling money? She could work in that poxy club to pay for herself for once.

He opened the doors to the building and was immediately impressed. Stars he knew well were artly displayed on the walls in light boxes, Leon Mendez among them. Sasha had all the northern talent, some of whom were now household names, no doubt thanks to her.

He walked across the polished floor, which was white and looked as though it had glittering diamonds set into it, and headed to the polished chrome work station in the centre. He signed the visiting book, giving his best wink and finger guns to the receptionist as she checked him in. She smiled tightly at him and turned away. He went to sit to wait for Sasha, and when he looked back, he could see the receptionist on the phone, giving him a sideways glance. She giggled, quickly stifling the noise by putting her fingers on her lips. She continued talking feverishly and then put the receiver down.

'Sasha will see you now. Through the double doors, straight through to the end of the offices, her door is right at the end.'

Greg nodded, standing slowly so she could take in his physique fully. He pretended to stretch, knowing that his fitted t-shirt would ride up, exposing his happy trial. 'Thanks, daarrlin',' he said, in the mock southern cowboy drawl he sometimes used to charm the ladies. She couldn't take her eyes off him, he could feel them on him the whole time he was heading out the door. He sauntered through the office at the other side, enjoying more adoring stares on his way through. He saw one of the office girls nudge her friend, and he threw them both his best panty dropper smile. He knocked on the office door with Sasha Birkenstock written on it.

'Come in,' Sasha trilled.

He walked in and saw that she was sitting at her desk. He went to smile at her, but her face was set hard. She looked mad. 'Hi,' he ventured, wrong footed by her frosty response to him.

'Sit down Greg,' she said, monotone. 'We need to talk. I've been checking into you, I do with all my new clients. Some troubling things came to light. Now, when Rory told me -'

'Rory!' Greg exploded. 'You can't believe a word that little div says, he's a moron. He's just jealous of me.'

'Huh! Jealous of you? I don't think so somehow. Don't you dare raise your voice in my office, either. I can have security here in a second, so don't push it. I know what you are Greg, you're a bully. A snivelling little weasel. I have known men like you all my life. I don't know if you've heard of my father, not many have since it's something I have taken great steps to keep my business from. Before he went inside, he had dozens of people like you on his payroll, all mouthy, narcissistic nobodies who thought they were better than everyone else. You have nothing Greg, your child is lost to you, you're on thin ice with your job, and you bully women. I'm here to tell you, you've lost.'

Greg was floundering, trying to make sense of what he said. He could only think of one word. Birkenstock. It had sounded familiar when they had first met, and now he knew why. 'Birkenstock. Your dad is Basher Birkenstock?'

Sasha pouted, a sly smile crossing her flawless features. 'The one and the same, and he looks after his daughter. He hates people like you too, and the thing about prison is, you can still have long arms. You can reach someone with those arms without even touching them. Here's your cheque.'

Greg looked at the envelope she had between her slender fingers and snatched at it like Gollum. Ripping it open, his face fell. 'What the hell is this? You promised me four times that!'

'I delivered too. Right to your ex. Apparently, you're a bit forgetful. You forgot that when you have a child, you have to pay for it. I rectified that for you, that's what's left. According to my court sources, your wages at the fire station will be garnished for the rest, so that's good to know.' She smiled at him sweetly, as though she was enjoying ripping him apart inch by inch. 'I kept my other promise too, I've got you a national ad campaign. You're locked in for the next two years, and they'll work around your job for further shoots. It's product placement, they have a whole range. It's a good contract, and as long as you leave them alone, do your job and keep your nasty little head down, we'll be good. You'll have more than enough money to pay for your child and live like the self obsessed douche bag you are.'

Greg didn't say anything, just looked at the cheque, and back to her.

'It's all signed off, you did it yourself - remember all the papers I gave you? Next time, maybe give them a read.' She looked down at the diary on her desk and ticked something off. 'Now, if you don't mind, I have another meeting.'

He didn't move at first, staring into space in front of him. Sasha could practically hear his dusty cogs whirring and gnashing against each other, trying to comprehend what has just happened. She pointed to the door. 'Greg, you can go now.'

He stood on shaky legs and stuffed the envelope into his jacket pocket.

'Oh, and Greg, the campaign went live this morning. Enjoy your new found fame!'

Greg left the office as meek as a mouse. He didn't look at anyone, though he could feel the eyes on him. He felt like he had just left his balls on Sasha's desk for her to use as paperweights. All that work and he had only got a measly few hundred quid. Rory was laughing at him somewhere, while Sarah was counting his money, HIS money, and he couldn't do anything about it. Basher Birkenstock was not someone you wanted to meet in a dark alley. Hell, even meeting him in broad daylight dressed as a unicorn would be hair raising. The man was an animal. He made Leon look like a weedy kid. He would have to just swallow it, keep his head down. He headed back onto the street, lost in his own thoughts as he headed to the nearest pub to drown his sorrows. He could at least celebrate his contract though. Sasha was a lot of things, but she knew her job. She signed him to keep him on a leash sure, but she would want to make money off him too. He was just thinking about the money he could have coming, when a lady caught his eye. She was staring at him intently as they headed towards each other on the pavement, each heading in the opposite direction. She was openly staring at him. They were about a foot away from each other when the woman tapped him on the shoulder. She was in her fifties, a smart twin set in lilac on top of a smart pair of black slacks. She had a matching purple handbag on her arm, and she pushed it onto her shoulder.

'I'm so sorry for your troubles.' She said sincerely, giving him one last pat before continuing on her journey. Greg whirled around to ask her what she meant, when he saw it. On the bus stop, in the billboard cover, was a new advert. It was a photo of him, wearing only tight light blue denim jeans, fashionably torn, and a smile. He looked amazing, but he didn't even take that in. What he did focus on was the caption. He was standing in front of a red background, and in huge white letters were the words I CAN'T GET IT UP.

He made a funny noise in his throat, like a strangled scream, and ran over. He tried to rip it off, but it was locked away in the advert partition. He couldn't get to it. He noticed that at the bottom was another line and a logo. The line read '...without Erectron' and the pharmaceutical logo. Greg pounded on the bus stop, making passers by jump. One young lad with a skateboard flinched.

'What the hell, man?' He jabbed Greg in the arm. 'It's not our fault you can't get it up, is it? Chill!'

The people at the bus stop burst into laughter, and Greg ran. He yanked the hood of his jacket over his head. Two years of this were going to be torture. He ran home to his mother's house with his limp tail firmly between his legs.

CHAPTER TWENTY-TWO

'Gill Ira Cohen, put that phone away right now!' His mother discreetly scolded. She was a pro at that, having perfected it over the years. She was a master at chewing someone out with a few finger jabs, facial expressions and whispered telling offs. Gill sighed and quickly hitting send on his text, put it into his jacket pocket before his mother had the idea to confiscate it. They were stood in the Jewish community centre, although it looked very different tonight. It had been laid out with tableclothed tables, elegantly backed chairs, fake candles at every table (The smoke alarm incident of 2015 had put paid to elaborate candelabra - Rosemary's eyebrows had never looked right since).

His mother pulled him across the room to their table, standing him next to where his father sat in his chair. Gill could see that Ira had a pair of earbuds in. The football was on, and Ira's love for Arsenal had obviously overruled his fear of being caught by his wife. He nodded to his son jovially, taking his hand in his and patting it with his own age worn one.

'Good luck son,' he muttered, as though he was about to face something much worse than a planned blind date. 'Soon be over, then we can all go home.' He made it sound like surgery. Testicle removal probably, since Gill felt as though his were currently sitting amongst the mints in his mother's clutch purse.

Life was amazing. Dinah and he were spending every day together, and he was deeply in love with her. She had moved in now, in the spare room, although some nights they did meet in the darkened hallways. They were taking it slow, but Gill knew she was the one. They had been spending their weekends sorting out her mother's house, the For Sale sign on the lawn outside. She was doing well, better in the rehab centre. She could speak better already, and physiotherapy and depression counselling were making her better still. Gill noticed that she looked a little lighter every time they visited. He hoped that seeing her daughter happy and no longer alone helped her find a little peace too.

Dinah was out with her aunt tonight, they had arranged to go for a meal, catch up. She had teased him mercilessly all week about tonight, but never moaned about him going. ‘If Kate Hudson walks in, and she's your dream date, what're you going to do then? You'll regret hitching your wagon to me. I shall be living in a cardboard box in some alley while you get off to Hollywood to live the high life.’

Gill had laughed, pulling her closer on the sofa and kissing the tip of her nose. ‘I said she was cute, once. You make me watch all these romantic comedies, you can't blame me for looking! If Kate Hudson walked in, I would tell her. 'Kate, I thought you were cute in that film, yes, but Dinah is the Princess Leia to my Hans Solo, so off you pop!'‘

Dinah giggled, rewarding him with a kiss. ‘Your mother would disown you. Anyway, she's not Jewish.’

Gill groaned. ‘Can I not just tell her, avoid the whole thing? I'll be in trouble anyway, for living with you.’

Dinah was already shaking her head. ‘Nope, you have to grin and bear it I'm afraid. We’re just housemates till then. Friends. You can tell her after.’

Her last text had told him to look out for scarlet women, and he had text her back with a laughing emoji, unable to write more under his mother's beady eye. She was scanning the room now, straight as a meerkat as she looked around the room at the sea of chatting people. Her face broke into a broad grin, and she pulled Gill in front of her. She licked her finger and ran it along his eyebrow.

'Eugh, Ma! No! I hated that when I was 6!'

'Shh!' She whacked him on the back of the hand and Ira chuckled behind him. Gill shot a look over his shoulder that could kill a man at ten paces, and Ira stuck his tongue out at him. He stood and headed to the bar, where a couple of other men were standing quietly and sporting their own secret headphones. 'She's here!'

Gill suddenly felt sick. This was it. He had to meet a woman he had no intention of dating, all under the watchful eyes of their families. 'Where?' he said, turning to look where she was.

'There.' Abela said, reaching to grab his face and reposition it. 'She's with her aunt, she doesn't have much family bless her. Her mum's been ill.' Gill's jaw dropped. There, chatting to a group of people across the room, was a woman in a beautiful red dress. Her hair was pinned up in loose curls, and she looked radiant under the fake candlelight. She turned to look at him, and he walked straight over, his surprised mother hot on his heels.

'Hi,' he said, holding his hand out. 'I'm Gill. I think you're my date for tonight. Apparently, we're perfect for each other.'

Dinah smiled and took his hand in hers. 'Hi, I'm Dinah. Apparently, we are.'

'You're dressed in scarlet, I see.' He leaned forward and kissed her hand. His mother made an odd squeak at the side of him, but he ignored her. He could see a woman he recognised from the photos as Dinah's aunt watching them with a happy look on her face.

'I am,' she said coyly. 'I had a hot date.' The look on her face as she gazed into his eyes made Gill's heart tense in his chest, and he couldn't hold it back anymore.

'I love you. Marry me.' He said, simply. Dinah's lip trembled, and a single tear escaped her eye and ran down her cheek.

'I love you too,' she said. 'You're my Han Solo. Yes.' They both kissed each other, slow and lovingly, till a huge thud broke the romantic moment. They both turned around and saw Abela out cold on the floor. Everyone ran to her side, but she was already coming to. From across the bar, Ira burst into a cheer, followed by a huge belly laugh.

'He shoots, he scores!' he shouted, and fist pumped the air. 'This is the best night of my life!'

Across the room, David sat with his mother. She slapped him on the arm, making him wince.

'See,' she said, pointing at Gill and Dinah, who were now being cuddled to death by a very over excited Abela and her friends. 'Why can't you be more like Gill?'

CHAPTER TWENTY-THREE

Rory put down the phone and looked at his dad across the club office. They were having a meeting about the handover, and Gill had just interrupted with a squeal ridden phone call.

'Gill and Dinah are getting married, he just told his mother.'

Doug's jaw dropped. 'Dear Lord, that's amazing!' He went straight for the drinks cabinet, pouring them a large measure. 'Not driving, are you?'

Rory shook his head. 'I'll leave my car here, get a cab.' He took the drink from his dad and held it aloft. 'To new beginnings!'

They clinked the glasses and took a long pull. His dad patted him on the shoulder. 'So, best man eh?'

'Yeah,' Rory nodded. 'He just asked me. I'm honoured.'

'You next kid.' They both headed to the large sofa, sitting down together.

'I think you will be up the aisle before me, Dad, unless Bunny doesn't want to?'

His dad looked nervous but said nothing.

'Dad, I was joking. Don't worry.'

'I loved your mother so much son, I never thought I could feel anything like that again. Bunny 's different, she gets it. I really am fond of her, but once was enough for both of us. We're just happy being in each other's company.'

Rory nodded. 'As long as you're happy Dad, I am.'

They hugged each other, and Rory marvelled at their new closeness.

'You only get so much happy son, and it has an expiry date. When you find a piece, you need to run hell for leather towards it and never let it go.'

There was a knock at the door, and Doug stood up, draining his glass. 'I'm going to go chat to Winston, get another drink. I'll be on hand if anything comes up.'

He opened the door and there stood Sarah. 'Winston said you wanted to see me, Doug? Everything okay?'

Doug pulled her into the office, whirling her around so he was in the doorway. 'Yes, I did. You have some things to talk about, and I don't want you to leave here till it's sorted. Frankie has the bar.'

He shut the door behind him, and they were alone. She looked mortified but hid it behind a stony face. Rory swallowed and patted the seat next to him.

'Sit down, please. Do you want a drink?'

'I'm on shift,' she spat, but she relented and sat down, crossing her arms. 'What did you want?'

He thought of his mother, all those years ago. He thought of the new Rory, and what disasters it had caused. He had kept the clothes, the car, the contact lenses, but he was very much the old Rory. The old Rory who had unknowingly, even to him, been in love with his best friend. He thought of what his dad had said, about chasing happiness and he knew he had to take his shot.

'When Belle showed us those pictures, that awful day, it proved something to me that I think I had known for a long time.' He put his glass down on the table and turned to face her. She unfolded her arms and put them on her lap.

'What was that?'

'Every memory I have ever had since Mum that has been worth remembering involves you, and Belle. We know each other inside out, and we work. I never realised how much you meant to me till I thought I might lose you. I hated Greg -'

'Not Greg again,' she groaned. 'He's gone, he can't get to us anymore.'

'I know that, let me finish.' She scowled at him, pouting. 'Put your lip away and let me talk.'

He saw the ghost of a smile cross her face, and his heart beat faster. 'I hated Greg, but it was more than him being a complete git, I was jealous. And when Nigel came along, and Tim...I...I didn't like it. I don't think you liked Sasha either, for the same reason.'

'I'll get on with her, I won't be awful. If she makes you happy.'

'Sarah! You're not listening to me! Shut up!' He reached for her hands and wrapped them in his, rubbing his thumbs along her palms. 'I'm not with Sasha, that's over. I'm trying to tell you that I don't want to be that person, and I don't want to date her. I want to be me, plain old Clark Kent again, and I want you.' His heart was thudding in his chest now, his whole face white hot. He could feel his palms get sweaty. *At least if I get shot down I can fake a heart attack. Or my own death.*

'I want you too,' Sarah muttered, and when he looked at her, she was smiling at him. 'Do you mean it Ror, are you sure you know what you're saying? I'm confused as hell already. I don't want us to mess this up, and Annabel really wants it which makes it worse!'

Rory took her face in his hands and kissed her before she could talk herself out of it. He kissed her passionately, telling her all the things he wanted to say, to convey all the feelings he had for her. She had been there under his nose the whole time, and he hadn't even realised. She wasn't his dream girl, she was the very real girl next door. Better than any dream. She was the woman who challenged him, drove him crazy, and made him the happiest man on earth. The woman he would marry, raise a family with. Give his mother's locket to. His Sarah.

She pulled away after a long time, breathless. 'Well, for Clark Kent, that was very frigging Superman.'

He laughed, pulling her in again. 'Shut up woman and kiss me.' They kissed again, him pulling her onto his lap to get closer to her. She wound her fingers in his hair, smelling the aftershave he always wore that felt like coming home.

'You mean to tell me,' she said between him lunging for her, 'that we could have been doing this years ago?' Rory grinned through his kiss as she undid his shirt buttons.

'Well,' he said, popping one of hers in return. 'I rather think Yeadon Primary looks down on these kinds of shenanigans in the playground.'

She pulled his shirt off and gasped.

'What?' he said, panicked that she was about to run screaming from the room.

'You've been working out,' she growled, straddling him. They kissed again, exploring the parts of each other they knew so well, and the parts they didn't.

Sometime later, snuggled up on the couch, sweaty and

blissfully happy, he kissed her on the top of her head as she laid cradled on his chest.

'I forgot to ask earlier,' he said, rubbing his fingertips along her naked back. 'Do you fancy coming to a Klingon wedding?'

THE END

Acknowledgements

Many thanks to Lisa Hall, Liz Barnsley and the lovely George for all their hard work at Manatee Books. I couldn't have found a better home for Rory, and I couldn't have parted with him to anyone else. In fact, Lisa had to prise him from my grasp to even publish this book! Their passion for him equals mine, and I couldn't be happier with the Manatee Journey.

As always, a massive thanks too to all my writer buddies, especially Lynda Stacey, who is always there with a kick up the arse and a wise word. Reason #874 why we are friends.

A massive mwah to all the book bloggers and cheerleaders out there, who keep us writers feeling so supported. You are all amazing.

As always, love and thanks to my family.

25552154R00134

Printed in Poland
by Amazon Fulfillment
Poland Sp. z o.o., Wrocław